UP

THE

MOUNTAIN

UP

THE

MOUNTAIN

AN ACT OF REDEMPTION

JEFF HAMMONDS

Book design: mycustombookcover.com

Printed in the United States of America

First Edition

ISBN: 978-0-578-67699-9 (Paperback)
978-0-578-67700-2 (ebook)

To the storytellers in my family who have played such an important role in my life.

To my wife and kids who knowingly and unknowingly influenced this book.

To all the students who read the story in various stages of completion and encouraged me to continue.

Chapter 1

Carol, Rob's mom, sat alone on the couch, lost in thought. How many days lately had she sat there without the energy to deal with the simplest of chores? Things were out of control, and she didn't know what to do. Her thoughts drifted to what Rob was like as a boy, how happy he was. Carol was only eighteen when he was born, far too young to have a child. She and Rob's dad were only kids themselves. They weren't ready for the responsibilities of raising him, and it took a toll on their marriage until, finally, Rob's dad could take it no more. He walked out, leaving Carol to raise Rob on her own. Then, at the age of twelve, when his parents told him of the pending divorce, Rob had gone into denial. He refused to talk about it, and as time went on he pulled deeper and deeper into his own world. By the time he was fourteen, his father had disappeared completely from his life, not even a call on his birthday.

Now as a seventeen-year-old, Rob was in complete revolt. Carol had known for quite some time that he was hanging out with the wrong crowd, but she had hoped that it would pass. Things, however, were only getting worse. Throughout his senior year, calls from the school became the norm.

"Rob wasn't in class today. Is he home sick?"

"Rob started trouble with another student, and you'll have to come pick him up."

"Rob's not performing up to his potential. Is there a problem at home we should know about?"

Carol was just glad that he had made it through school and graduated. Many days she thought that it wasn't going to happen.

Now, though, she had no control over him at all. Without school, every semblance of structure had left Rob's life. At times, he could still seem like that pleasant young boy he used to be. She didn't know what to do. What could she do? An opening door brought her out of her daze. She looked up to see Rob walking across the room. She could hardly believe this was the same cute little boy she remembered–the straggly unkempt hair, the sleeveless blue jean jacket over the white t-shirt, and the emotionless expression on his face–this couldn't be her son.

Without even looking in her direction, he called, "I'm going out," as he walked past her, seemingly trying to not acknowledge her.

Carol stood up from the couch and said hesitantly: "Wait, Rob. Where are you going?"

"Down to Oceanside." He stopped and turned toward her momentarily as his hand searched for the door knob.

They looked more like brother and sister there together in the room. They each had sandy-blonde hair and a slender build, the same blue eyes.

"Wait, Rob. Don't tell me you're going down there. That place scares me. Everyone down there is looking for trouble."

He stepped toward his mother and said, almost in a threatening tone, "If you don't want me to tell you I'm going down there, then don't ask."

Carol—trying to keep her composure, trying to keep from just breaking down, trying to keep from just giving up—said, "That's not what I meant. Please, Rob. Don't go down there. I'm afraid you'll get hurt."

Rob walked over to his mother, smiled, and put his hand on her shoulder. "Hey, that's where all my friends go, and we aren't going to get hurt. All we do is hang out. How can we get hurt doing that? Don't worry about me. I'm a big boy. No one's going to hurt me."

Rob's mother looked at him pleadingly, "Please don't go, Rob."

Then he turned angry as quickly as he had turned nice. "Well, I'm going, and you can't stop me." With that, he turned and walked out of the house. The slamming door brought a finality to his words and a silence to the room.

Carol sank slowly down onto the couch and started to sob. "What am I going to do?" she thought. How had she so totally and completely lost control of her son?

...

Rob went out and got into his car, an old Chevy Nova that he had bought from a friend. He was going to pick up his friends; it was their Friday afternoon ritual. He'd pick them up, and on the way to the ocean they'd get high. Then they'd go walk along the beach near the pier. They'd try to pick up girls, usually without any luck, harass any Blacks or Mexicans they saw, and fight anybody who would stand up to them. Rob wasn't as gung-ho a skinhead as some of his friends. He didn't have a swastika tattooed on his arm like Danny. But he did agree with his brothers. 'Why don't they all go back where they came from?' he often wondered.

When he stopped to pick up Steve, he knew as soon as he saw him that he was already wired. Steve jumped onto the bumper of the car, looked over at Rob, smiled, and said, "Aw, man, I'm ready to kick some butt tonight. I'm wired and ready to go." He let out a howl, and Rob laughed as he started the car.

"Let's do it," Rob said. He pulled out a joint and the party was on. By the time they picked up Joe and Danny they were both feeling a good buzz. Joe had the beer. He was the only one old enough to buy it, so that was always his contribution.

On the way to the beach Steve continually stuck his head out the window, hollering at passing cars. By the time they arrived, they were all stoned. They hopped out and started to make their way down the boardwalk that followed along the ocean. People were strolling along, enjoying the beautiful afternoon. Occasionally a girl would pass by on rollerblades, and Rob and his friends would holler at her to stop.

Then Steve put out his arm and stopped his friends. "Hey, hey, look who's coming. Joe, get out your phone and get a video of this." They all looked down the walkway and saw a dark-skinned man with long hair walking arm-in-arm with his girlfriend. Joe quickly got out his iPhone and stepped back to video the encounter. As the couple neared Rob and his friends, Steve stepped in front of them.

"What are you doing here? Nobody wants you on this beach," Steve said as he glared at the two young lovers.

The couple tried to ignore him and walk on by, but Steve stepped in front of them and blocked their path. The young man then looked up at Steve who was glaring at him menacingly. "Hey man, I don't want any trouble. We're just trying to enjoy the sunshine."

"Why don't you go walk along the beach in your own country?" Steve said as he pointed his finger at the young man's chest. He stepped toward the young man, seeming to grow larger as he drew closer and almost growling as he spoke.

Now the young man started to get angry as he stepped toward Steve and said, "This is my country. My ancestors were here long before you white men showed up and thought you could buy it all. Why don't you go back to your country?" He moved closer, eyeing Steve, but his girlfriend was pulling on his arm, trying to get him away.

"Come on, John," she begged. "Let's go."

John and Steve glared at each other until John, at the prompting of his girlfriend, relaxed and started to turn away saying, "Ah, you're not worth it." Then Steve, like a wild animal sensing just the right moment to attack, swung his right fist around, catching the young man flush on the face as he turned to leave. Like a pack of wolves, Rob and his friends all charged as soon as his punch landed. That first blow buckled the legs of the young man, and he quickly found himself balled up on the ground, defenseless. His girlfriend backed away, screaming. Others around them started shouting.

The scene quickly turned into chaos. Rob and his friends started kicking the young man as he lay curled up on the ground, begging for mercy. Joe was laughing and encouraging them all, screaming, "Kick the f'ing crap out of him. Go back home, asshole," as he continued to video the whole encounter.

Caught up in the frenzy and excited by the moment and Joe's encouragement, they kept kicking the young man as he lay there on the sand until all at once they all seemed to realize that he wasn't moving. Steve was the first to speak. "Come on! Let's get out of here."

They took off running down the beach. Rob glanced back and saw that no one was coming after them, but they kept running until they came to the parking lot where he'd left his car. They all slowed, out of breath. Steve let out another scream, laughing and punching the air. "Man, that felt good. Did you see him go down? That was one good punch."

They were laughing and talking excitedly as they got in the car, their adrenaline still flowing. Then, just as Rob started to back up, police cars materialized out of thin air, rushing into the parking lot and blocking his escape. The policemen quickly jumped out of their cars and dropped behind their doors with their guns drawn shouting, "Driver first, get out of the car! Now! Keep your hands up so we can see them. Get down on the ground face down. Now!"

It seemed that before Rob could even begin to focus on what was happening to him, he found himself lying face down on the asphalt with his hands cuffed behind him. Policemen were everywhere, and he could hear one of them on his radio calling for an ambulance, saying that someone was badly hurt and may be dying. All of the blood ran out of Rob's head when he heard those words, and he thought he was about to pass out. What had he done?

...

The next thing he knew he was sitting in a jail cell. Everything had been moving so quickly that he still wasn't thinking clearly. The events of the past hour were a blur, a foggy haze that had to be a dream, that just couldn't be real. But the reality of the bars, the cold hard floor, the smell, couldn't be ignored. As much as he tried to shake off the fog, to make it all disappear, he knew that it was all true.

This wasn't the first time he found himself in a jail cell. But he was soon to find that this time was much more serious. The young man they had attacked was in the hospital in critical condition. Due to the severity of the beating, the district attorney could charge them with attempted murder. The city was tired of the violence on the beach, and they wanted it to be known that it would not to be tolerated. They were tired of the skinheads on the beach scaring off the tourists. The citizens were demanding that something be done, and now they had someone in custody–Rob Phillips.

Chapter 2

✦

When the phone rang at 10:28 p.m., Carol immediately sensed that it was about Rob and that it wasn't good news. It wouldn't be the first time the phone had rung on a Friday night with news about Rob. She hesitantly picked up the receiver. "Hello?"

"Ms. Phillips?"

"Yes."

"Are you the mother of a Rob Phillips?"

"Yes." Carol's heart was beating so furiously that she was afraid she was going to pass out.

"This is Sergeant Donaldson with the Oceanside Police Department. I'm calling to inform you that we've arrested your son."

With those words the receiver nearly fell from Carol's hands.

"Oh my God." She began to sob and her hands shook uncontrollably. "Can I come pick him up?"

"No ma'am. Rob will be with us at least for the night. He'll have to go before the judge in the morning, and the judge will set bail."

"What happened?" The words seemed to be spoken by someone else. Carol could hardly think, hardly stand.

"Your son and his friends assaulted a young man down at the beach. Because of severe nature of the assault, the likely charge is attempted murder. The young man is in the hospital right now, and all these boys had better hope that the charges aren't upgraded to murder."

"Oh my God, no." With those words Carol began to cry uncontrollably.

"Ms. Phillips," the officer, though, continued matter-of-factly, "you may either call or come down in the morning, and by then we'll know when Rob is going to get in to see the judge."

"What will happen then?" Carol said as she tried to calm herself.

"Well, the judge can either set bail, or he can refuse to set bail and hold the boys until the trial. If he sets bail and you can make it, your son will be released to you."

"Do you have any idea how much it will cost?"

"Ma'am, I have no idea." He wanted to say that he hoped it would be extremely high because he was sick of these punks coming down and causing trouble in his town. He was sick of making arrests only to have the punks released the same day, sick of never seeing an end to his job; but he kept this information to himself.

Carol felt faint as she looked around the room for a chair before she fell down. "Oh, what am I going to do?"

The young sergeant had seen this situation too many times in his career, a young man out of control, a family torn apart. He wanted to tell her to just let the boy stay in jail. Don't even bail him out; he'd only break her heart again. Instead he said, "Ma'am, come in and speak with the judge in the morning, and he'll give you your options. If you have any more questions, you can call the precinct tomorrow and ask to speak to me. Remember, it's Sergeant Donaldson."

"What time should I come in?" Carol said as she tried her best to keep her composure, but the spasms and sobs continued.

"Ma'am, you'll just have to call down to the county lockup in the morning. They should be able to tell you something. Or you could call your attorney this evening. He may be able to find out something for you. Do you have an attorney?"

"No, not at all. And I don't have the money for one either. What am I going to do?"

"Ma'am, I'm sure you know they'll appoint one for your son if he can't afford one. That's about all I can tell you." He paused for a second. "Ma'am, I'm sorry."

He WAS sorry, sorry she had a delinquent son she had to deal with, sorry he had to make these calls; but he wasn't sorry the boy was behind bars. That is where he deserved to be. He wished he would stay there, but there was little chance of that. These punks were ruining his city, and he wished he could put all of them behind bars.

...

The following morning Carol called the courthouse, and she found out that Rob would be brought before the magistrate at eleven o'clock. He would set bail and the arraignment date for when Rob would enter his plea.

At eleven o'clock Carol was seated in the courtroom when they led Rob in. Shock overwhelmed her when she saw him walking into the room in leg irons and handcuffs.

"Oh God," she thought. "He's only a boy." She got up to meet him, but the bailiff stopped her. Rob was led over and seated in front of her. His eyes never left the floor. He couldn't bear to look at his mother as she leaned over and hugged him.

Rob had hardly sat down when the bailiff called the courtroom to order and announced his case. The magistrate looked at Rob for a moment and said, "Son, I've read your case and due to the violence of the attack and that this is not your first offense, I am setting bail at $10,000."

With those words Carol's heart sank. Where could she get that kind of money? Then the judge continued. "I also see that you have requested a public defender. I will review the information provided me and give you my decision by this afternoon. Your arraignment is set for a week from Thursday at ten o'clock in this courtroom." He slapped his gavel down and that was it.

Rob hadn't gotten to say a word. He had thought about how he was going to explain to the judge how sorry he was, and how he had only been drinking, and he'd never do it again. But it was already over. There was nothing he could say, nothing he could do.

He turned to his mother and said, "Mom, please bail me out. I can't take it in here."

Carol was starting to cry again. "I don't have that kind of money, Rob."

"Talk to a bail bondsman. It should only take a thousand or so."

"Rob, you know I don't have that much money."

"Can you borrow it from your brother? Please Mom." Rob was near tears himself. He had to get out of there. But the bailiff was already taking him by the arm to lead him away. He was pulled to his feet, and the bailiff started him toward the door.

Carol wanted to grab him and pull him back, tell them there had been some kind of mistake. Her son couldn't possibly be involved. He was only having some problems right now. He was a good kid, her only boy, her only child. What was she going to do? And then he was gone. She watched the door close behind him as she stood there helplessly. What was she going to do?

...

Carol sat alone in her house. Her world was collapsing around her again. Why did these things keep happening to her? Where had she gone wrong? She had no choice but to call her brother, but it seemed that the only time she talked to him was when she had problems, which was more frequent as of late. Oh, God, how would she tell him?

She finally got up the courage and picked up the phone. It was one of the hardest things she had ever done, explaining to her brother everything that had happened. She told him everything the judge had said, and she finally explained to him that she needed to borrow $1000.00. His quick reply came like a slap in the face.

"No, Carol. I won't loan you the money. Let him sit in there till the arraignment. It will do him some good. Give him time to think. But let me tell you what I will do. Get me the number of the judge and let me talk to him to see if Rob could come live with me as part of his probation. A boy shouldn't be growing up in all that mess."

"What?" Carol nearly dropped the phone. She couldn't believe what she had just heard. Her brother lived on a ranch up in the mountains in Montana. She had grown up there too but had left it long ago, too long ago.

"Yeah, let him come live with me, Carol. Working on this ole ranch would straighten him out in no time. Why, he might not want to return. Carol, why don't you come too? I mean it."

She couldn't believe what she was hearing. Her mind was swirling with thoughts and questions. Could it even be possible? "No, I couldn't come. My life, what there is of it, is here now. But do you think the judge would let Rob come live out there? Oh God, that would be great. I don't know what to say to you. But, Ron, I don't have the money to get him there." Reality quickly set back in on Carol.

"Don't you worry about that at all. Just get me the judge's number, and I'll take care of it."

Carol began to cry again. It seemed to her that's all she did lately. "I don't know what to say."

"Don't say anything, Sis. Just get me the number and call me back."

She hung up the phone in disbelief. She couldn't believe what her brother was willing to do for her. But what would Rob think? And would the judge even allow such a thing? Well, she would just have to see. At least she had something to hope for now.

...

Later that day the courthouse called to inform Carol that Rob had been assigned a public defender. The attorney's secretary called shortly thereafter and told Carol that the attorney would meet with Rob and her the next day at two o'clock in the courthouse. Then they would decide what steps should be taken. Carol asked what their options were. The secretary told her that the attorney would discuss that with her tomorrow, but the options were really whether they should fight it, throw Rob on the mercy of the court, or try to plea-bargain.

Chapter 3

The next day Carol found herself walking down the halls of the courthouse again, looking for room 413, which was where she was supposed to meet the public defender and Rob. When she entered the room, the first thing she saw was a young man who couldn't have been out of law school for more than a year. He rose from his chair, smiling, and walked toward Carol with his hand extended. "Good morning. You must be Ms. Phillips. How are you today? I'm sorry. That's a dumb question. I'm sure you've had better days. Come in; sit down. Rob hasn't made it here yet. They should be bringing him in any minute now."

Carol sat down and listened while he prattled on. She thought how this might be amusing under different circumstances. He hasn't even told me his name, she thought. This is the man who is supposed to defend my son? He's obviously more nervous than I am. "Excuse me," she finally said. "I'm sorry, but you haven't told me your name."

"Oh." He rose and stuck out his hand again. "I'm Mr. Harrison, Bob Harrison. I don't think I'll ever get used to that Mr. thing." He smiled nervously at Carol. "Now, where was

I? Oh, yes. I've read over the police report. Unless Rob has something completely different to tell me, it's a pretty cut and dry case. The state has lots of witnesses. They even have the video that one of the boys took with his phone. I don't see any other option but for Rob to plead guilty."

Tears welled up in Carol's eyes. "But what does that mean? Will he go to prison?"

Then the door to the back of the room opened and Rob walked in. The sight of him in leg irons and handcuffs was enough to drive her insane. She jumped up and ran across the room to him. He turned his face away from her. He didn't want to look into her eyes. He looked completely disheveled, like he hadn't slept since he had gotten there. But a quick glance at his mother told him she looked worse. He could tell she'd been crying, probably hadn't stopped since his arrest, he thought.

The lawyer asked the guard if he could remove the cuffs and leg irons now, which he did without complaint. The guard said he'd be right outside the door and would escort Rob back to his cell promptly at three o'clock.

Carol stood there holding her son, quietly crying. Mr. Harrison thought briefly how she didn't seem old enough to be Rob's mother. He also wondered where the father was, but that wasn't his concern right now; and they didn't have much time.

"Excuse me, Ms. Phillips, Rob, but we need to get busy. We only have about an hour here to come to some type of decision." They all sat down and Mr. Harrison began again. Carol was waiting for just the right moment to tell Rob about her brother's plan. She knew that it was the best option, if they could do it. But she wasn't sure how Rob would feel about it. However, if it came down to going to prison or going to Montana, how could he say no?

"Now, Rob," Mr. Harrison began again, "I've read the police report, and your statement. Unless there's something you haven't told them, I don't think you have any other option but to plead guilty because I don't see much chance of you ever winning in court. Is there anything you can add to the information I have here?"

Rob looked down at the floor and said, "No, there's nothing I can add. We did it, and we got busted. That's all there is to it. Is the guy still alive?"

Rob had to ask. It's all he had been thinking about. But it wasn't that he was concerned about the young man. He was only afraid of facing a murder conviction, not just attempted murder.

"Yeah," Mr. Harrison said. "They say he's going to make it. He's really beat up though." Mr. Harrison turned to face Carol now. "But there is more bad news. I imagine he will end up suing these boys for his medical bills."

Carol slumped even further down in her seat and lowered her head. What else could happen to her? Financially, her life was already in shambles. She barely made enough to make ends meet. Well, usually they didn't. Now what would she do?

"But," Mr. Harrison continued, "we shouldn't worry about that right now. We need to decide what we are going to do at this time. Rob, I think you're going to have to plead guilty, as I said. That really isn't debatable. But we still have other options to think about. We can try to plea bargain for a lesser charge. According to the report, you weren't one of the boys who instigated the beating. However, under the law you are just as culpable for going along with it. But the judge might be sympathetic and let you plead to a lesser charge. We could go in and ask to speak to the judge in his chambers. I've already spoken to the assistant D.A. in this case, and he mentioned he might be amenable."

"What does that mean?" Rob asked.

"It means he might be willing to work something out."

Both Rob and his mother looked up at these words.

"Now don't get me wrong. I'm only saying the sentence might be lighter. You're still in a lot of trouble here, Rob. I'm only trying to get some options for you. It may not work at all. It's really out of our hands. But I think we can get you a little less prison time if we try to work something out."

The words 'prison time' took about everything out of Carol. She knew that Rob's only chance was to go to Montana, so now seemed like as good a time as any to Rob's mother.

...

"Umm, may I speak?" She began.

"Of course, go ahead."

"Well, I haven't mentioned this to Rob yet, but I have a brother who has a ranch up in Montana. He told me that if the judge would allow it, he'd like for Rob to come live with him and work on the ranch."

"What!" Rob jumped up out of his chair. "I'm not going to live in Montana."

"Now wait a minute, Rob." Mr. Harrison stood up too. "This might be a great opportunity, and I think the judge just might go for it. What would you rather do? Go to prison or live on a ranch with your uncle?"

"Well, how long are we talking about here?" Rob asked.

Mr. Harrison was now pacing around the room, his mind racing. "Well, Rob, it might not be an option at all. It will be up to the judge and D.A., but I think if we were to go in with a formal appeal, it just might work. As far as a time period, that will be completely up to the judge." He turned toward Carol. "We'd need to get a statement from your brother, possibly a statement from law enforcement in Montana saying that your brother is a citizen in good standing in the community. He is, isn't he?"

"Oh, yes. He's a well-respected rancher. I know we could get everything you need." Carol was beginning to get excited thinking this might work. Finally, something good might be happening for a change. But Rob was sitting there in a daze.

"We'd probably need to make some type of arrangements with probation. I really don't know how that would work. But I can find out. Rob, I think we should do it. What do you think?"

Rob's head was still spinning, but he didn't see any other option. "Let's do it, I guess."

Carol grabbed Rob and hugged him. "I'll go right home and call my brother."

"Well, not too quickly here." Mr. Harrison spoke up. "I'm supposed to meet with the D.A. later this afternoon. Let me kick the idea around with him and see what we need to do. I'll give you a call later this evening and tell you what I've found out. Then you can call your brother."

...

Around six o'clock that evening, the phone call finally came. Carol's hands were shaking when she picked up the receiver.

"Ms. Phillips? This is Mr. Harrison. How are you doing this evening?"

Carol wanted to say, 'How do you think I'm doing?' But she tried to remain calm and polite. "I'm doing as well as can be expected, I guess. Tell me, what did you find out?"

"I have to say, things actually went better than I expected. The D.A. wants to sit down and talk to Rob himself. He also wants to talk to your brother. There are lots of details to work out, and we'll still have to write up a formal proposal and submit it to the judge. Furthermore, it's the judge who will make the final decision, but he'll usually go along with the district attorney's recommendation in these cases. And luckily for Rob, he hasn't turned eighteen yet, which gives the judge a lot more leeway in the sentencing. Here's where things stand right now. Ms. Phillips, are you still there?"

She still couldn't believe what she had just heard. She hadn't made a sound since Mr. Harrison had begun to speak. "Yes, I'm still here. Go on."

"Okay, this is what the district attorney will recommend to the judge. Rob will receive a six months' adjudicated sentence with a three-month review and three years of probation."

Carol's voice was trembling, and she was beginning to get scared again. "What does that mean, a six months' adjudicated sentence? Does he have to stay in jail six months?"

"No, no. I'm sorry Ms. Phillips. Let me explain. Adjudicated kind of means at the judge's discretion. It means the judge will allow Rob to stay with your brother for three months, and then he'll want to visit with him again, speak with your brother and find out how things are working out. If things are going well and with your brother's approval, Rob will be able to spend another three months there. At the end of those three months, he'll be allowed to return to California; but he'll be on probation for another three years, which means he'll have to stay out of trouble for a long time. Rob must also be made aware that your brother will be able to recommend that he be returned to jail if things are not working out."

"That's how it stands right now if the judge will go along with everything, that is. I'm going to write up the proposal to submit to the judge, and we already have a meeting with him set for Monday at ten o'clock. It will be in the judge's chambers at the courthouse. Hopefully, if everything works out, we can get this wrapped up at that time, and Rob won't have to go to trial at all.

"The district attorney will be contacting your brother to work out any details with him, and everything should be ready to go by Monday. So if you don't hear anything else from me, I will see you Monday morning at 9:45 a.m. in the lobby of the courthouse."

Carol hung up the phone still dazed from all that was said and still unsure how to feel about everything. It did sound promising, though, she assured herself.

Chapter 4

On Monday morning, Rob found himself seated in the judge's chambers with his mother, Mr. Harrison, an assistant district attorney, and the judge. The judge was a stern-looking man in his mid to late fifties. He had been sitting behind his large desk, reading the documents before him, since Rob had entered the room. The walls of the room were covered with shelves of books. No one in the room spoke. They all seemed to be waiting for the judge to give them permission to breathe in his presence. Finally, he looked up from the papers and said, "So you're Rob Phillips."

"Yes, sir." Rob replied.

"I've been reading over your case and the documents given to me by both the district attorney and your attorney. They each seem to believe that it would be in your best interest to ship you off to live in Montana. What do you think of this arrangement?"

"I'll do whatever you tell me to do." Rob answered.

"I don't think that was my question, son," the judge replied sternly. "You WILL do whatever I tell you to do. What I want to know is whether you think this is in your best interest."

"No, I don't think it will be in my best interest 'cause I'm sure I'll hate it as much as I would going to jail," Rob replied.

The judge leaned forward and looked intently at Rob and said, "Son, I'm tired of seeing your kind here in my courtroom. If I thought at all you'd enjoy your stay in Montana, I'd send you off to jail right now. But I spoke with your uncle, and I think this might actually do you some good. So I'm going to follow the recommendation of both your lawyer and the district attorney and allow you to go live with your uncle. But let me tell you, if you show up in my courtroom at the end of the first three months with anything but a good report from your uncle, I will sentence you to the maximum allowable punishment for your crime. Do you understand me young man?"

"Yes, sir," Rob replied meekly.

"Good. You must be at your uncle's house by the first of next week. That gives you one week to get your affairs in order here, which I am hesitant to do; but I'm going to. Do you understand that? And do you think you can stay out of trouble for one week, young man?"

"Yes sir," Rob replied.

"Good. Then, you will remain in your uncle's custody until the time of your return, and I shall see you here in my office in three months. Until the time of your departure you must remain in the custody of your mother at all times. You are not to go out alone under any circumstances. And you are not to have any contact with the other defendants in this case. Is that clear?"

"Yes, sir."

"Good. That is all."

Everyone started to rise when the judge spoke one last time. "Oh, and you should know that I will be speaking regularly to your uncle, and I expect to receive only good reports. One bad report, just one, and you'll be back here facing me before you can blink an eye. Good luck to you, Ms. Phillips."

"Thank you, Sir," was the only reply she could get out of her mouth.

"Well, it looks like I'm going to Montana," Rob said as they exited the judge's chambers.

Chapter 5

One week later Rob found himself sitting in a truck in Montana with his uncle Mr. Larson. Within minutes of leaving the airport, they were traveling across the rolling plains of Montana on the two-hour drive from Bozeman to Mr. Larson's ranch up in the mountains. As Rob watched the scenery pass quickly by the window of the truck, he couldn't help but think that the plains were as empty and as barren as he felt. The vastness around him made him feel even more alone. If only he had known, though, of the richness of life that existed in those plains, he might have felt a little less alone. For a while they rode along in silence. Finally, Mr. Larson spoke.

"Rob, I know you don't want to be here, but I want to tell you that you are welcome just the same. I expect for us to get along fine. As long as you do what I ask and treat me and my family with respect, you and I will never have any problems. I want you to know that I will always treat you with respect and dignity. Is that fair?"

"Yeah, that's fair," Rob answered, but he was thinking, 'I'll do what the f... I want.'

"I'll expect you to help out around the ranch. You'll help Sylvia with the chores, and she'll be able to show you what to do. I think if you give it a chance, you just might like living on the ranch."

'Yeah, right,' Rob thought. 'There's about as much a chance of that happening as there is of me staying here the whole summer. First chance I get, I'm gone.'

"I also want you to know that I haven't told any of them exactly why you are here. I just told them that you had gotten into a little trouble back home, so you wanted to try living with us for a while."

Rob looked out the window and saw an antelope running alongside the truck off in the field to his right. Mr. Larson saw him watching it and said, "There are lots of antelope around here. You don't see them up around where we live because the elevation is a lot higher. But we do have a lot of deer, elk, and even bear."

"There are bears around your ranch?"

"Yes; in the spring we lost two calves to a bear. I think he's moved on, though, 'cause I haven't seen any sign of him in a while. But they can travel a pretty large range, so he might come back. We have lots of coyotes, a few cougars, and we're not that far from Yellowstone, so it's always possible that we could see a timber wolf. That was a big deal up around our parts when they decided to release timber wolves back in Yellowstone. But I really don't see it as a problem. They'll never be in great enough numbers to ever do any damage to our herds. And we lose more to the cold weather than we ever would to wolves anyway. I think it was more just people's fear of them than anything else. Oftentimes, the fear of the unknown is far greater than the actual danger it presents. I don't see how anyone could honestly argue that they are liable to cause an economic burden on anyone."

Rob couldn't remember the last time an adult had talked to him in this way. Most of his dealings with adults in the last few years had only been arguments. He found himself wanting Mr. Larson to keep speaking, but he didn't know what to say.

Their surroundings had been changing for quite some time. The rolling plains were disappearing, and there were trees everywhere now, and everything was much greener. Aspen groves were woven through the evergreens on the mountainside, which gave two quite distinctive looks to the forest. There had been mountains around Bozeman, but the mountains now seemed much larger. They were now at a higher elevation, so a coolness hung in the air, which made every breath seem crisper. Mr. Larson had turned off the air conditioning in the truck and had rolled down the windows quite some time ago. Rob had never seen the sky as blue in California as it was here. There wasn't the haze in the air that he was used to seeing and had grown up thinking was natural.

There were wisps of white clouds in the sky. Some thunderheads loomed out over the mountains. Dark billowing clouds rose high in the air above the peaks. Rob saw lightning flashing across the jagged ridges above them. Mr. Larson noticed him watching the lightning and said, "There are almost daily thunderstorms up on the peaks. I love to sit out and just watch the lightning up there. Sometimes it's quite a show."

The mountains still had a lot of snow on them. Mr. Larson explained to him that in early June there was still snow on the mountains and that it would never completely melt up on the highest peaks all summer long.

Ron turned off the road and pulled up to a gate. Before them lay a beautiful, green pasture. A split log fence ran along the roadside. And the entryway was a large wooden gate like something Rob had seen in the Westerns on TV. Above the gate was a large beam with "Rockin' G Ranch" carved into it. "Well, here it is," he said as he handed Rob a key. "Go open the gate. It swings out toward the house. After I've driven through, close it and lock it." Rob got out, swung the gate open, and closed it after Mr. Larson had driven through.

The driveway went on for at least a quarter of a mile. At the end of the drive, Rob could see a large house. Off to the right about a hundred yards was a large barn, and beside the barn were several smaller barns and outbuildings. As they neared the house, Rob could tell that it was a log cabin. "Cool house," Rob said as they pulled up in front.

"You like it? I designed it and built it myself. Well, that is, with the help of quite a few other people. All the logs came from trees right here on the ranch. My wife and I hand-selected every log."

"Cool," Rob said awkwardly. The house was shaped in an octagon, with one large chimney in the center, two other chimneys protruding from the sides, and a wrap-around porch encircling the home. The land right around the house was flat, but only a few hundred yards behind the house the elevation started to rise.

Rob pulled out his cell phone and quickly glanced down at it. Mr. Larsen noticed him and said, "You can just put that thing away. You're in the middle of the mountains here, and you won't find any reception anywhere around here. That's just a glorified watch out here. It's a pretty one though." Mr. Larson smiled as he hopped out of the truck.

As Rob got out of the truck, he noticed that back behind the barn there was a large pen with a wooden fence. Inside the pen was a girl on horseback. She was doing a kind of figure eight around some barrels that were set up. Mr. Larson saw Rob watching the girl and said, "That's your cousin, Sylvia. It's about time you two met. You should have met long ago. I don't know why we didn't have you out here years ago. She's practicing for the rodeo. She's a barrel racer, quite good, too. Have you ever seen barrel racing?"

"No," Rob replied. "I've never seen a rodeo, and I don't really care to either. I don't really think it would interest me at all."

"Well, Sylvia will be competing in a number of them over the summer. You might change your mind after you've seen one."

Mr. Larson reached through the open window and tapped on the horn of the truck a couple of times and waved at Sylvia when she looked in their direction. She waved at them, rode over to the side of the pen, and dismounted. Quickly and efficiently, she removed the saddle from the horse and threw it over the railing of the corral. Then she undid the bridle, patted the horse's neck, and slid a lead rope loosely over its head. She grabbed a brush that she had placed near the gate earlier and started brushing the horse down.

"Come on; I'll take you over to meet your cousin. We'll get your luggage later." Mr. Larson started walking toward the corral, and Rob fell in behind him. He hadn't noticed before how big his uncle was. He was at least six feet two inches tall with broad shoulders. He looked right at home on a ranch, with his cowboy boots and hat. Rob still couldn't believe that this was his mother's brother or that his mother had once lived in this hellhole.

As Rob drew near, he could see that Sylvia was tall like her father, and she was dressed out in western wear: blue jeans, cowboy boots, a western shirt, and a cowboy hat.

Great, Rob thought, just what I need, a cowgirl.

But when they were only a short distance apart, Rob could see that Sylvia was strikingly beautiful. She had long, jet-black hair that was tightly braided; dark, tanned skin; and dark, brown eyes. But Rob realized immediately that she knew all about him. She stared at him apprehensively for a moment and then continued to brush the horse, and Rob thought that she even seemed a little bit frightened by him. You should be, he thought.

"Sylvia, I want you to meet your cousin, Rob," Mr. Larson said. Sylvia didn't even look up from brushing the horse.

"Nice to meet you," she said, and she kept brushing the animal.

"Sylvia!" Mr. Larson said, and she could tell by his tone that he wanted her attention. "I want you to take Rob and show him around. Have him go with you to put the horse in the barn and then take him up and show him around the house."

"Yes sir," she said. Her father had already told her that he wanted her to treat Rob as she would a friend and relative, and she knew that was what he expected. He told her that even though Rob had done something wrong, they must treat him with respect. Her father said that they should teach Rob through their example. She knew that he was right, but she also knew it was going to be hard. I can be kind, she thought, but I don't have to like him.

She untied the lead rope from the corral and started walking toward the barn. "Come with me, Rob," she said as she was leading the horse away. They started walking toward the barn. She was on one side of the fence and Rob was on the other.

"I'll see you all up at the house. Rob, I'll go ahead and grab your luggage and carry it up to your room." Mr. Larson called.

"Thanks," Rob called as he walked quickly along trying to stay up with Sylvia. They walked along in silence for a moment, and Rob knew that Sylvia was ignoring him.

...

When they were near the barn, she finally broke the silence. "I'll lead the horse in around on the back side of the barn. If you want to go in, there's a door around in the front that ought to be open." With that, she walked the horse on around to the back. Rob saw the door Sylvia had talked about and thought he'd go on in since he'd never been in a barn before.

He entered into a wide, open area in the center of the barn. On each side were stalls. Sylvia was leading the horse in through the large open doors at the other end of the barn. She led the horse over to one of the stalls and put it inside.

"So, is that your horse?" Rob asked.

"Yes. That's Rising Star. The horse in the stall next to her is mine also. That's Golden Boy."

Rob looked in the stall at a big palomino. "I can see why

he's called Golden Boy. Why do you call the other one Rising Star?"

"If you look at her, she has a star on her forehead; and when I was younger, I just thought it was a neat name. She was born here on the ranch when I was seven. Dad gave her to me on my eighth birthday," Sylvia said.

"Are these the only two horses you have here on the ranch?" Rob asked.

"Oh, no. We have over a hundred horses. They're all out in the pastures. We only keep a few here in the main barn. "

"A hundred?"

"Well, this is a horse ranch, ya know," Sylvia said.

Rob pulled out a pack of cigarettes, took one out, and stuck it in his mouth.

Sylvia looked over at him and said incredulously, "What are you doing?"

"What's it look like I'm doing? I'm lighting a cigarette. You want one?" Rob pulled another one out of the pack and stuck out his hand to hand it to her.

"You can't smoke that around here. My dad won't allow it. He doesn't let anyone smoke on the ranch."

"Well, let's just not tell him, and he'll never find out." Rob said with a little smile. Then he took a small step toward her, and lowered his voice and said harshly, "I'm not going to tell him and neither are you."

With that, Sylvia turned and started marching toward the house, taking Rob completely by surprise.

"Hey, wait," Rob said; and he started walking along quickly behind her. "Hey, I'll put it away if that's what you want." Sylvia kept right on walking toward the house. Rob ran up beside her and said, "Hey, there's no need to get so mad about it. I was just kidding. If your dad doesn't want me to smoke, I won't. Come on, Sylvia. Slow down."

Sylvia stopped and turned toward Rob. He could tell that she was angry. "Look, you're here as our guest. I am not going to have you threatening me. If you ever do that again, I'm going to have my father ship you back to California."

"Hey, come on. I wasn't threatening you. I was just playing around. Can't you take a joke? I'm sorry." Rob was using all his usual tricks he used on his mother, playing the bad guy and then being nice to make her feel guilty; but Sylvia wasn't falling for it at all.

She continued to stare at him. She wasn't his mother, and she resented him being sent there; so Rob's tricks weren't going to work with her at all. "Let's get something straight right now," Sylvia said. "I know a joke, and I know when someone is trying to con me. My dad told me to be friendly to you, but he wouldn't want me to let you do something wrong. So don't ever ask me again. Do you understand that?"

Now Rob stood there staring at her. He wasn't used to a girl standing up to him, let alone telling him what to do. He wanted to tell her what she could do with all her dad's rules, but he didn't want them to start watching him too closely. He needed to just play it cool and wait. If he were going to be able to get away from this place, he needed to have them relax around him. He had to make them trust him and think he liked it here.

"Yeah, I understand."

Then Sylvia turned and started toward the house without saying another word. Rob fell in behind her and followed her up to the house. As they entered through the front entryway, Sylvia's mother greeted Rob immediately. Her hand was extended as she walked toward him.

"Why hello. You must be Rob. It's nice to meet you. You know, I knew your mother long before she moved to California."

She shook hands with Rob, and he was surprised to see that she seemed to be genuinely glad to meet him. He was perplexed by her kindness, and he found himself at a loss of words. Finally, he managed to tell her that it was nice to meet her too.

"You knew my mother when she lived here?" Rob asked.

"Why I sure did. Ron and I started dating when she was still in high school. I've known her since she was a teenager." She smiled and said, "I'll have to tell you sometime what she was like back then. Now you just make yourself right at home here. If there is anything you ever need, you just ask us. Okay?"

"Sure," Rob replied. He liked her immediately. There was something nice about her, something reassuring.

"Ron has already put your luggage in your room. See the stairs over there? There are three bedrooms and two baths upstairs, so you'll have your own bathroom. Your room is the one at the far end of the hall. If you want to go up and check it out, you just go right ahead. Now there's a chest in there for you to put your things in and you've got a closet in there too. You are going to be here for a while, so you just make yourself at home. You might want to rest a little while after your trip. I know you've come a long way, and I bet you're tired. Just go on up, and Sylvia will come get you when it's lunchtime."

"Thanks," he replied. "I think I will go rest for a while. Thanks a lot."

Rob went on up and found his suitcases lying on the bed.

He began to unpack his things and to wonder what he had gotten himself into. At least, he thought, this is better than that jail cell. After he had unpacked his things, he lay back on the bed and in no time the chaos of the last week took its toll on him.

...

Whoa, he thought when he looked out his bedroom window. He could see the snow-covered mountains just out behind the house. It looked like he could reach out and touch them. When they had arrived, the clouds had been covering the peaks; and he hadn't seen them. He sat there staring out the window, amazed at the view.

Soon, though, he couldn't believe how tired he was. What a week, he thought. What was he going to do? When he closed his eyes, all that had happened over the past week started circling around in his mind. His thoughts were whirling. He opened his eyes and looked out at the mountains again. Soon, though, he began to relax more than he had in a long time. For some reason he felt safe. He gently closed his eyes and drifted off into the deepest sleep he had had in quite some time.

Chapter 6

It seemed like no time at all until a knock at the door awakened him. When he opened it, he found Sylvia standing before him.

"Mom told me to come get you and show you around a little bit before lunch, and she said you might want to freshen up a little before you eat."

Sylvia showed him around the house, and finally she took him back to a room off to the side. As she reached for the door, she said, "This is my grandfather's room." She knocked gently and then opened the door and walked into the room.

Sylvia led him across the room to an old man whose skin was wrinkled with age, whose hair was as long and thick as her own but was a stark gray. He sat near the fireplace where a small fire burned. An old Indian blanket, like the ones Rob had seen at the flea markets back home, was draped across the lap of the old man. He just seemed to be staring into the fire.

When Rob was a short distance from the old man, he turned to look at Rob. Their eyes met and locked momentarily, but Rob found he had to look away. He had to look away because he felt as though the old man had seen him naked, had looked into his very soul, had known more about him from that brief glance than he knew about himself.

"You are angry," the old man spoke softly.

"No," Rob replied a little too quickly, a little too loudly. He laughed nervously, trying to regain his composure. Then he turned and walked away, trying not to let on how much the presence of the old man disturbed him. He walked out of the room with Sylvia walking quickly behind him.

"Where are you going?" Sylvia asked. "You walked away before I could introduce you. That was rude."

"I don't know. I just didn't want to stay in there. What's the deal with the old geezer, anyway? He looks like an Indian." Rob said as they walked into the living room. He was trying to get his composure back, not let Sylvia know how much the presence of the old man had disturbed him. He didn't like other people seeing or knowing his feelings. They were personal.

"He is my grandfather, and he is an Indian, or Native American as we like to be called. He's a full-blooded Lakota," Sylvia replied.

"Why would I want to meet him? I don't have anything to talk about with that old man, and what did you mean 'as we like to be called?'"

"Of course, if he's Native American, that makes me one too. My mother is full-blooded also, which makes me half Native American. Didn't you know? And I never said you would want to meet him, but you are going to be living in the same house as him; so you could have at least been friendly."

"He lives here, too?"

"Yes, he does. He's lived with us for as long as I can remember. And I am glad he lives here. He's always there when

I need someone to talk to. He always seems to know what I'm feeling and know just the right thing to say. It's almost as if he knows me better than I do. I don't know what I'd do without him. But I don't know why I'm telling you this. It's obvious you don't care."

"You're right. I don't care how nice he's been to you. I really don't care about talking to a wrinkled old man. I know he doesn't know what I'm feeling, and I could care less what he's feeling. So why don't you just leave me alone, and you don't have to worry about what I'm feeling either. I know that's what you want."

"Fine, and don't tell me what I want. You wouldn't have any idea what someone like me would want. You know where everything is now. Lunch will be ready in ten minutes. Don't be late."

"Fine. I won't." And with that Sylvia walked away and left Rob standing there alone.

Well, he thought, things are off to a great start here. I'm just not going to be able to make it through the summer. What am I going to do?

Rob decided that what he needed to do was to go have a cigarette. He walked out of the house, and deciding he didn't want Sylvia to catch him again, he walked on out into the woods that were only a short way from the house. It was only ten minutes to lunch, so he didn't go far. As soon as he thought they couldn't see him from the house, he lit up a cigarette and inhaled deeply.

'Man, that girl is going to drive me crazy. I've got to get out of this place,' he said to himself. Rob leaned back against a tree to finish his cigarette. As he leaned back against the tree, something came over him. He put the cigarette out and listened for a moment.

It was so quiet, peaceful. He couldn't hear any cars, any sounds associated with humans at all. All he could hear were the birds singing and the wind whistling through the trees. It had hardly seemed like he had been there long at all when he realized that the ten minutes had passed. He hurried back to the house to have lunch in his new home, without realizing that a new life was upon him.

Chapter 7

Rob's first week on the ranch was a hard one for him, but he was finally starting to get into the routine around the house. Rob couldn't believe that he had to get up and do chores each day. He had never done that before in his life. It seemed to him that they had a routine for everything. Every morning he had to get up and help feed the animals, clean out their stalls, and make sure that they all had water. Rob wasn't used to routines. He had had very few of them in his life, at least for as long as he could care to remember, unless he could consider going out and partying with his friends a routine.

Now, finally, it was Saturday night. The day had been a lot more relaxed. He still had to get up that morning and take care of the animals. Mr. Larson had explained to him that there were no days off when it came to living on a ranch. You always had to take care of the horses. After the morning chores, the rest of the day had been a peaceful one.

Mr. Larson had told him that it was all right if he wanted to go exploring around the ranch. He said there was a lot more to it than Rob had seen around the house. So Rob had walked out into the woods above the ranch. Mr. Larson had explained to him that their land went all the way up into the mountains, and above their land was all National Forest. He told him that he could explore all he wanted as long as he paid attention to where he was and to make sure he could make it back to the house all right. He said to stay inside the fences and not go out into the National Forest land until someone else could go with him.

"There's a lot of rugged country out there," Mr. Larson had said, "and I wouldn't want to have to send out a search party for you your first week here. Let's give it at least a month 'til we have to do that, all right?" he said with a laugh.

Rob wandered up into the trees above the ranch. As he walked along he tried to keep sight of the ranch behind him. The evergreen forest began to get denser as he left the pasturelands around the ranch behind. Soon, though, he made his way into a grove of trees that were much different than the evergreens. The leaves were a light green and the trunks of the trees were nearly white. The leaves of the trees rattled in the breeze. It was pleasant sitting there in the grove, the wind whistling through the trees.

He found a spot in the grove where the grass grew long, and he lay back on the ground and watched the clouds roll by overhead. He actually enjoyed himself lying there, all alone in the trees. Who would have ever thought it, he wondered to himself. In no time the day had passed, and he had to make his way back to the house for dinner while there was still plenty of light.

Soon they were all sitting at the dining room table having their evening meal. Everyone seemed to be in a pleasant mood, and Rob felt good about the week. He had worked hard, but he had actually enjoyed it at times. Still, he couldn't wait to get back home. But he was already thinking less about running away. I think I can put up with this place for a while. No need to break my probation. One week of servitude down and twelve to go, he thought. Well, twelve weeks until I have to go back and see the judge. Maybe the judge will decide that I've learned my lesson and let me stay in California. Nah, no chance of that, Rob thought. That man is going to make me stay here the full six months.

He had already started to enjoy their dinners together, too. Usually, at home, he just scrounged around for whatever he could find to eat. Rarely did he and his mother ever sit down and eat together. Well, they never did any more, he thought. He couldn't remember the last time someone had cooked for him, especially someone who was a good cook.

Now it was time for the dinner routine. Everyone took his plate to the kitchen from the dining room, and everyone helped clean up the kitchen.

Rob carried his plate to the sink, rinsed it off, and carried it to the dishwasher- his nightly routine. Then he noticed the others were walking toward the old man's room at the back of the house.

"Come on Rob," Mr. Larson called. "It's story time."

"What?" He replied.

Then he found Sylvia taking him by the arm and leading him toward Grandfather's room.

"Saturday evening is story time. Grandfather will tell us stories, and we'll clean the kitchen later. Dad doesn't like for Grandfather to be kept up too late, so we clean the kitchen after we have heard his stories."

"What type of stories does he tell?" Rob asked.

"You'll see. Actually, we never know what he's going to tell us. I'm never really sure if they are true or not, but I always enjoy them. They seem to be true, though."

Rob felt a little uneasy. Even though he had seen the old man all week long, he still felt weird around him. He felt like the old guy was always looking at him, staring through him.

Everyone entered the old man's room. Rob could tell that he had been waiting on them. The chairs were set up in a circle with the old man as the focal point. As usual, a fire was burning in the room, but Rob noticed a difference immediately. First, Rob was certain that some type of incense was burning. Also, the old man was dressed differently. He seemed to be dressed up for the occasion. His long hair was braided. There seemed to be something ceremonial going on, something almost ritualistic.

The room was quiet. No one was speaking. Rob wanted to ask what was going on, but it seemed out of place for him to speak. So he decided to just wait to see what would happen. When everyone was seated, all eyes turned toward the old man. When Mrs. Larson spoke, it startled Rob. He had been expecting the old man to speak.

"Tell us about when you were young, Grandfather."

Rob thought it was strange that Mrs. Larson always called her father, Grandfather. He thought that he needed to ask Sylvia about that sometime, but he knew now was not the time. Now everything was silent again. The old man was looking into the fire as if he had not even heard his daughter. Rob had waited as long as he could, finally deciding that the old man had not even heard what was said, and he was just about to repeat it when the old man looked up and began to speak.

"When I was young, I was an Injun."

"What? You're still an Indian." Rob spoke without thinking about it. He was used to just blurting out whatever popped into his head. That's what everyone he knew did, but now he sensed immediately that he had done something wrong. Everyone was staring at him, everyone, that is, except Grandfather.

The old man continued to look into the fire, and he said, "Forgive him for that outburst. He is young and new to our customs. He will learn."

Then he turned and looked directly at Rob.

"When stories are being told, no one speaks but the speaker. Now I will continue with my story. I lived on the Reservation with my family. Things were bad on the Reservation. There was little work and even less to eat. The men of the tribe had a council meeting, and it was decided that those of us who could should go out and seek work among the white men so that our families would not starve in the winter. In that day there was much logging going on up in the mountains. I knew that they were looking for good men, strong men who would work for long hours. So my brother and I set out to find work in the logging camps.

"We had to search for several days before we found a camp that would hire Injuns. The first few days we had to walk several miles from the camp to the area where we were allowed to cut trees. The white loggers were given the area nearest the camp, which also had the best trees. But it wasn't long before the boss saw that my brother and I were cutting down the most trees each day even though we were not in the best location. Then, being a good businessman, he moved us up to the area where there were larger trees.

"But the other white men resented this move. They didn't like us working alongside them, especially since we worked harder than they did. I could feel the tension building, and I knew that it was only a matter of time before there would be trouble.

"We had been there less than a week when one night my brother and I were sitting out near the fire before we bedded down for the night. Some of the white men had been drinking, as they did every night. But this night they were being a little louder than the other nights, and they sounded angrier.

"I heard them as they came toward my brother and me. I heard one of them yell, 'Hey, Injun.' We had found, though, that it was best not to even answer them. So I sat looking toward the fire. But this night would be different. I only remember my brother jumping up and yelling. The axe handle caught me squarely in the back of the head. I did not wake up until the next day. I found myself lying on a cot in the boss man's cabin. My eyes were swollen and my ribs hurt badly. I could not raise myself off the cot. When I tried to get up, the boss man told me to lie back down. He said that I had a couple of ribs broken. He told me that my brother was dead. They had split his skull open with the axe handle. He was dead by the time the doctor got to the camp. They had beaten us only because we were different, because we were Indians. They did not consider us to be humans. I never even found out who did it. No one would tell an Injun anything. And the white man's laws didn't even punish them. We were just Injuns."

"But not all punishment comes from man. The Great Spirit knew, and he is always just. Now I am an old man, and they are not; I am at peace, and they are not; I am a human being, and they are not."

The old man had finished speaking, but no one moved and no one spoke. Rob sat there thinking about what the old man had said. He looked around him and saw that the others were all sitting silently, each with his head bowed, deep in thought. The only light in the house was from the fire in the hearth. Rob looked at the light dancing around the room from the fireplace.

There was something surreal about the moment. Rob's thoughts started to drift. He remembered his third grade class. They had studied Native Americans. He looked about him and was suddenly taken back when he thought he saw what was the inside of a hogan. The old man was wrapped in his blanket sitting beside the fire.

His mind continued to drift, and he soon found himself at the beach. He could hear the waves crashing in the distance. The scenery was beautiful, peaceful. But something was wrong with the scene. He knew that he should have felt serene, but he was anxious. Soon he began to hear noises about him. People were shouting. He seemed to be apart from the scene, watching it but unable to do anything about it. Then he saw a group of young people in front of him. These were the people who were shouting. They were all so angry. Then he saw that he was part of the throng, and he knew what it was.

"No!" His shout startled the others in the room. Mrs. Larson jumped up and ran over to him. His breathing was forced, and he was sweating. Rob looked around the room, a little disoriented. For a brief moment he wasn't sure where he was. Mrs. Larson put her arms around him, trying to calm him down.

"Rob, are you alright? What's wrong?"

Rob looked at her for a moment. Her arms were so

comforting. For a moment he wanted to just lean against her and tell her everything that had happened. He wanted to tell them all what he had done. Then he pulled away from her and said, "Nothing. I guess I fell asleep and was dreaming. I saw a beach and. . . . Oh, never mind."

Everyone was standing around him, staring at him. He stood up quickly and said, "Hey I'm fine. I'm sorry if I disturbed you. I'm going to go on up to my room if that's okay."

"Sure, Rob. That's fine," Mrs. Larson said.

As he was walking out of the room, his eyes caught Grandfather's. For a moment Rob thought, he knows. He knows everything. That's why he told that story. But then he thought that was just crazy, and there's no way the old man knows. How could he? Still, he found it difficult to break away from the old man's stare. Finally, he turned and said, "I've got to get to bed." And with that he left the room.

Chapter 8

When Rob awoke the next morning, he had a strange desire to speak to the old man. He had slept restlessly through the night. Strange dreams had haunted him, and for some reason he wanted to tell Grandfather everything. He wanted to tell him about his life, about the mistakes he had made. He had to speak to him. When he walked downstairs, he immediately knew that something was different. Everyone seemed to be unusually busy for this time of morning. No, that's not it, he thought. They are always busy at this time. Something was just different.

Rob saw Sylvia sitting at the kitchen table, and then it dawned on him. She was in a dress. He hadn't seen her in anything but blue jeans.

"Good morning, Rob," Sylvia said halfheartedly. "How'd you sleep?"

Rob was puzzled by this question. She had never asked him this before. He was even more puzzled because this was the first night he really hadn't slept well. "Not well," Rob replied as he continued to look at her in a perplexed way. "Why do you ask?"

"I don't know. Does it really matter? I guess I was just trying to start a conversation if that's all right. Why didn't you sleep well?"

"I had a bad dream, I think."

"What do you mean, you think?" Sylvia asked. "Either you had a bad dream or you didn't."

"Well, I can't remember it real well. I just know it bothered me, and I didn't sleep well because of it."

"You should talk to Grandfather. He interprets dreams, you know."

Rob started to ask her what she meant by that when Mrs. Larson walked into the room.

"Oh, I'm glad you are up," Mrs. Larson said as she entered. "We were just about to come wake you."

"What's going on?" Rob asked.

"Well, we have church, and we have to leave in about an hour; so you have plenty of time still to get ready," Mrs. Larson said.

"Church?" Rob replied incredulously.

"Yes. Now you just get something to eat. Then go on and you get ready. I don't know if you brought your church clothes. We forgot to tell your mother for you to bring them. If you didn't, you just wear whatever until we can get you some," Mrs. Larson continued.

"I'm not going to church," Rob said, and he immediately realized he had said it a little too forcefully. The family turned to look at him. He felt embarrassed under their steady gaze. "I mean. I wouldn't feel right. I don't remember ever going to church before. I don't even believe in God." Again, Rob sensed by their expressions that he had said the wrong thing.

"Look, no offense, but I wouldn't feel right in a church."

Mr. and Mrs. Larson looked at each other for a moment. Then Mr. Larson said, "Rob, I don't feel right about this. I really think you should go to church, but I also don't think someone should be forced to go. I wish you'd come with us, but I'm not going to make you. I do think it would do you some good to come along."

Rob looked at Mr. Larson for a moment. There was no way he was ever going to go to church, but he also didn't want to offend Mr. Larson any more by telling him that. He needed to stay on that man's good side. "Well, maybe I'll go sometime, but I want to get used to being here a little more first."

"Well, I guess you'll be alright here," Mrs. Larson said. "Grandfather is back in his room if you need anything. He doesn't go to church either," Mrs. Larson said with her usual smile and genuinely nice personality.

"Your father doesn't go?" Rob asked.

"No, he says he's always in church. I don't know what he means by that, but there's no point in asking. I wouldn't understand his answer anyway. Well, you just make yourself at home, Rob." Then Mrs. Larson turned and they went about their business. Rob ate his breakfast in silence.

Mrs. Larson hummed as she worked about the kitchen. She seemed pleasant enough, but Rob couldn't help but feel he had insulted them. Well, he thought, he wasn't going to church for anyone. He'd rather go ahead and get shipped back to jail than go to church.

Rob soon found himself alone in the kitchen. Mr. and Mrs. Larson had told him goodbye as they had left for church. Sylvia walked out without even looking at him. It was the first time he had felt alone all week long. Someone was always around the house it seemed. Even when he went to bed, he had noticed that he still did not seem alone. He found this odd as he thought about it. Back home he seemed to be alone a lot, and he felt alone a lot. Even when he was with his friends he would feel alone. Here, there seemed to always be noises around the house, friendly noises, welcoming noises. At his home, there were always noises, but they didn't seem to be comforting noises. There were sirens going, or horns honking, or people shouting or talking too loudly.

Rob stood there pondering all this, lost in his own thoughts, when he realized he was no longer alone. The old Indian stood across the room, staring at him. It startled Rob, and just as with each of the other times he had been in the old man's presence, he seemed to be at a loss for words.

"You seemed disturbed," Grandfather said as he walked slowly toward Rob, never taking his eyes off him.

"Uh, no, I was just thinking," Rob replied.

"Come! Walk with me," the old man said as he turned and started out the door. Before Rob could object or even reply, the old man disappeared.

Well, Rob thought to himself, I guess I'll follow the old man. I sure don't have anything else to do.

By the time he got out the door, Grandfather was twenty yards ahead of him down a small trail. Rob thought about calling to him to wait up but quickly realized that the old man would never slow. Rob couldn't believe how fast the old Indian traveled down the trail. He ran a little bit then fell in line behind him. For twenty minutes the old man followed along the path without ever saying a word. They made their way across the pasture and were now heading across some broken ground. There were boulders here and there, and the ground was becoming more rugged.

The trail climbed steadily as they headed away from the house. When Rob glanced behind him, he couldn't believe how much they had climbed since they left the flatland around the ranch. He could see the house in the distance. Before, there had been pastureland; now there were trees. They were not yet into the forest, but they were getting close. Around them were pine trees. Rob knew what those were, but in front of them was the grove of trees Rob visited the day before.

As they neared the grove, Rob began to hear the wind whistling through the trees. They seemed to shimmer and speak as the wind blew. Rob found himself entranced by the trees, so much so that he almost ran into the old man who had stopped in front of him.

"What are these?" Rob asked the old Indian. I came up here yesterday when I went for a walk by myself.

"These are aspen trees. We are in an aspen grove. Come, over there is a place where we can sit."

He led Rob into a cluster of rocks. The dirt was worn as though he had been there many times before. The old man walked over, sat on one of the rocks, and pointed to another.

"Sit. This is my church," the old man smiled at Rob and for the first time Rob found himself relaxing in the old man's presence. "This is where I come when I want to think, when I want to listen to the wind. Can you hear it?"

"Yes," Rob replied as he thought, how can I not hear it?

The old Indian seemed to be listening intently. He was

silent for several moments, and then he asked, "What is it saying to you?"

"What?" Rob asked somewhat taken back by the question.

"What is it saying to you?" the old man asked again.

"I don't understand," Rob replied.

"Ah, then you must listen longer." Then the old Indian bowed his head as if in prayer and closed his eyes.

This guy is just too weird, Rob thought. Thoughts were racing through his mind. What was he doing here? What did this old man expect him to do? How was he ever going to make it in this place another three months before he could return home?

Then, the leaves caught Rob's attention. The aspen leaves were sparkling and changing colors in the breeze. He realized he could hear the leaves rattling and almost swishing in the wind. Is this what the old man was talking about? He began to listen intently. Slowly, without Rob even realizing it, a calm overtook him that he hadn't felt in ages. He relaxed. When was the last time he had truly relaxed? He found comfort there in the aspen grove.

This would become the first of many mornings Rob and the old Indian would come to this place in the woods. For over an hour the two sat in silence, each comfortable in the other's presence.

Rob hadn't even realized how much time had passed until Grandfather stood and said, "We must return. The others will be home soon. But before we go, I must show you something."

Rob followed Grandfather back among the rocks to a place where there was an overhang. On the rock wall below,

Rob noticed strange drawings all along the wall. He had seen Indian drawings much like these before in books.

"Cool," he said as he walked up to get a closer look.

"This is a sacred place among my people," Grandfather told him. "Always respect this place and show reverence while you are here. This is a place of power, a holy place, a place where you will find peace."

Rob looked more closely at the drawings. "How old are these? What do they mean?" He asked.

"No one knows. They have been here for hundreds of years, and what they mean, I do not know. But I do know that it is a spiritual place. The spirits of my ancestors are here. You may come here only if you will show respect to my grandfathers."

"Oh, I will," Rob said, somewhat in awe of what he was seeing.

"This is also a place of renewal. I come here for my own spirit to be renewed. I come here to have visions, to talk with my ancestors. I come here to think and to let my spirit soar. Did you feel your spirit soar my son?"

"I did feel something," Rob replied. He paused and thought for a moment, "Ya know, I felt very relaxed and at ease."

"Good. Come, we must go." And without another word the old man turned and started back down the path. Rob realized as they were walking back toward the house that he had never spoken to the old man about last night. But now it didn't seem as important to him. He couldn't believe how at ease he felt in this old man's presence as they walked back toward the house. Just a few hours ago he had felt strange standing near the old Indian. Now, only a short time later, he felt a bond with this man that he could not explain or even understand.

They walked all the way back to the house without either of them saying a word.

...

Not long after they got home, the Larsons returned from church. The day passed quietly, but all day long Rob kept thinking about Grandfather and the morning they had spent together. He kept thinking about the night before and how he had not slept well. He felt, for some unknown reason, that he had to go talk to the old man. Finally, Rob walked quietly into the back room where the old man sat staring into the fire.

"May I speak to you?" Rob asked.

The old man turned and looked at Rob, then silently nodded and motioned for Rob to sit down.

"I had a disturbing dream last night," Rob began.

"That is to be expected; you have led a disturbing life." The old man spoke so softly that Rob found himself leaning forward to hear him.

"Who told you that?" Rob asked defensively.

"You told me that."

"I've never told you that; I've hardly ever even talked to you, other than this morning, and I didn't tell you anything about my life."

"You told me that with your eyes, with your mannerisms, with your soul. And you see, the inner self sometimes reveals what the outer self refuses to see. That is why you are having the disturbing dreams. But that is a good sign. Before, you refused to listen to yourself; now you are hearing for the first time. So, you see there is still hope for you." The old man smiled at Rob, and Rob relaxed.

Then he looked down for a moment and said, "When I told Sylvia that I had a bad dream, she told me to come to you and that you could help me understand it."

"Well," Grandfather began, "there is some truth to what Sylvia has said. Some say I have been blessed with the power to interpret dreams, but for a dream to be interpreted correctly, one must know the dreamer well. Of course, I do not know you well, but I may be able to help you. Tell me your dream."

Rob thought for a moment, trying to decide how to begin. "Well, I was back home in California, and I was walking along the beach."

"The same beach that you saw last night?" Grandfather asked.

"Yes, I believe so." Rob continued. "And I kept passing buddies of mine, but they kept ignoring me. I tried to speak to them, but they refused to listen to me. They would look the other way as they passed me."

"How did you feel? What did you want to tell them?"

"I felt hurt, angry. I don't know what I wanted to tell them. No one would stop, so I never actually said anything to any of them. But I know their faces were angry. They were talking loudly, yelling at other people as they passed. Finally, someone walked up to me and looked at me." Rob fell silent for a moment, wondering how to go on, wondering how Grandfather would react. Finally, he looked into the old Indian's eyes and said, "It was a young Native American man we had beaten up at the beach. He just stood there staring at me. He didn't say anything, and I didn't say anything to him. I don't know how long he stared at me, but it seemed like forever. Finally, he just smiled at me. And that is all I remember of the dream. I think I woke up at that point."

"How did you feel when you woke up?"

"I think I was disturbed."

"You think? It is important. You must remember. And what made you disturbed?"

Rob tried to remember everything he could. He knew that the dream had bothered him. It still did, but what exactly bothered him he was not sure. But there was something else about the dream that was comforting on some level. The more he thought about it, the more he found something pleasant about the dream too. He told this to Grandfather, and Grandfather began to smile at him.

"I now understand your dream." Grandfather said.

"Tell me, Grandfather. What does it mean?" Rob asked. He quickly realized he had called the old Indian "Grandfather," but it seemed right, felt right; and Grandfather had not reacted at all.

"I think you have begun to understand the dream too. And that is good. You are beginning to try to understand who you are instead of just doing whatever you want and not thinking about your actions. Once you do that you are on your way to becoming a man. Now tell me, what do you think your dream means?"

"Well, I know what was so disturbing to me. All of my old friends ignored me. They walked by and didn't even try to talk to me. I think this bothered me."

"But have you stopped to ask why they ignored you?" Grandfather asked. "That is a very important point in understanding your dream. Yes, they did ignore you, and that bothered you. Now tell me why."

"I don't know why," Rob said.

"Tell me this. When you return home, do you want to be friends with them again?"

Rob looked at Grandfather puzzledly for a moment. Then the realization hit him. Grandfather began to smile as he noticed Rob's reaction.

"No, I don't want to be their friend."

Grandfather continued to smile and said, "Now you see that you were ignoring them. They were not ignoring you. You are no longer the same person as before. In the dream you said that they were angry. You thought they were angry with you. They were not. They were angry only because they wanted to be angry. They are angry at everything, not at you. Just as you were angry at everything when you arrived here. But that anger is leaving you, and that is good."

Rob thought about this, and he knew that Grandfather was correct. He had been angry at everything and everyone. He knew that he blamed others for his problems. But now he realized that he shouldn't. As Mr. Larson had once said, if there are problems, you don't complain. You work to fix them. And he realized that he needed to work to fix his problems and to stop blaming others.

Grandfather smiled as he saw Rob looking off, deep in thought. This young man is learning, he thought. Then they each sat silently in the room, comfortable in the other's presence. A weight seemed to lift off Rob as he sat there. What a strange sight they made, the old Indian man and the young white man, each sitting quietly, deep in thought, the fire casting strange shadows about the room. Not a word was said as they sat there over the next hour.

Chapter 9

It was now well into summer, and Rob was getting used to working around the ranch. He now enjoyed his life, working with the horses, the land, and especially his time spent with Grandfather. Rob had just gotten down to breakfast. He was smiling, thinking how amazing it was that he was getting up at 6:30 in the morning in the summer. But he had quickly discovered that if he wanted to eat breakfast, he had to get up when everyone else did. He also found that he liked getting up early. There were so many things to see and hear at that time of the morning. Everything on the ranch seemed to be alive. The air outside was so clean and fresh in the morning. And it always amazed him that he needed a sweater on in the morning in the middle of the summer.

Mr. Larson looked up from his pancakes and said, "Good morning, Rob. How would you like to earn some extra spending money today and tomorrow?"

"Doing what?"

"Helping me get the hay in. Today we're going to cut and rake it, and tomorrow we'll bale it."

"What would I have to do?"

"Well, today I'll be on one tractor, and I will go through and cut the hay. You will come along behind me on the other tractor and rake it into rows so that when we bale it tomorrow, it'll already be raked and ready to bale. Normally, we let the hay stay out in the field a few days after its cut to let it dry out. But this summer it's been so dry we won't have to."

"Why do you have to let it dry out?"

"Well, if you don't let it dry and you put it in the barn too early, it can spontaneously ignite."

"What?" Rob looked at Mr. Larson like he was trying to pull his leg. "You mean it will catch on fire?"

"Yes, it'll just burst into flames like you'd put gasoline on it and set it on fire. Hay is very combustible anyway; but when you put it away when it is still green, it starts a chemical reaction and the heat inside the bale gets so intense that it will just catch on fire. Have you ever noticed the steam coming out of my compost pile?"

"Yes."

"Well, that's caused by a chemical reaction too, much like what would occur with the hay. But the difference is that the hay is so combustible. The heat will reach a point where it is just too great, and it will burst into flames."

"Have you ever seen it happen?"

"No, and I don't want to either. My barn is so old and that lumber so dry that if a fire were to start, the whole thing would be gone in a matter of minutes. Do you think you'll be able to drive the tractor all right?"

"Sure. It can't be that difficult."

"Yeah, Sylvia normally drives the other tractor, but she's

going to be spending the day preparing the horses for the competition. But she'll help us bale tomorrow. We'll get a couple of other kids here tomorrow to help."

"What'll we be doing tomorrow?"

"Well, I'll drive the baler, and Mrs. Larson will drive the truck pulling the trailer. Sylvia and her friend Mary will be on the trailer. The boys will walk along and pick up the bales and throw them up on the trailer. The girls will stack them neatly."

"Why neatly?"

Mr. Larson laughed, thinking how much Rob had changed and thinking of all the questions he was asking, "Well, just so we can get more on there."

"How long will this take?"

"All day, probably. I hope to get three hundred bales out of that field. So I expect you guys will be throwin' bales all day long."

"How much do these bales weigh?"

"Well, you're lucky that it's been so dry. They'll probably only weigh 40 to 50 lbs. If the bales are wet and a little green, they can weigh upwards of 80 lbs."

"You mean you expect me to throw 40 to 50 lb weights around all day tomorrow? You've got to be kidding."

"Well, I'm going to be paying you 20 cents a bale to do it, so just think that every five bales you and your friend throw is a dollar. So if we get 300 bales tomorrow, you'll earn $60.00. And I'll pay you $40.00 today for driving the tractor. By tomorrow evening you'll be $100.00 richer. Next week we'll be gettin' in my other hayfield, and I expect your arms and back will have just about recovered by then."

Mr. Larson smiled and got up from the table. He didn't tell Rob to come on. He didn't say anything. He just walked out the door and headed toward the barn.

Rob realized he'd never even told Mr. Larson if he would do it or not. He smiled to himself as he realized that even though Mr. Larson had asked him if he wanted to do it, he really didn't have a choice. Mr. Larson expected him to do it. Rob felt a little bit of pride in himself because Mr. Larson had asked him to help. He felt like he was a part of the ranch now, and he had to assume some of the responsibility for taking care of it. And $100.00-- that was more money than he had seen in quite some time.

Rob liked talking to Mr. Larson. He always treated Rob like a man. He always explained things to him and didn't talk to him like he was a kid. He quickly finished his pancakes, ran out the door, and headed for the barn. Mr. Larson was already hitching up the mower to one of the tractors. Mr. Larson pointed over toward the side of the barn. "You see that piece of equipment over there with all the wires sticking out? That's the hay rake. Let me show you how to drive the John Deere real quick like, and you back it up over there; and we'll hook the rake up to her."

Mr. Larson explained all the controls on the tractor to Rob. It wasn't that complicated at all, and he had ridden on it a couple of times when Sylvia had driven out to the back pasture. Mr. Larson told him to go ahead and start it up and run it up and down the driveway a few times to get used to it while he greased up the equipment. After stalling it a few times, Rob quickly got used to the clutch, and he headed on up the driveway. He played around on the tractor for a few minutes. Then he backed it right on up to the rake and shut off the engine.

"Good job!" Mr. Larson called out from over at the other tractor. "Now come on over here and help me finish hooking up this one. Rob walked over and helped Mr. Larson align the shaft running back to the mower and in a matter of minutes they had it hooked up. Then they walked over to the rake and hooked it up.

"Alright now, Rob. You'll want to get a hat and a jug of water before we head out. Then we'll drive the tractors on out to the pasture, and I'll show you how to rake hay. We'll probably be finished by lunch; but if we aren't, we'll take a break and come on back here to eat. Go get your hat and water and meet me back out here."

Mr. Larson kept working right up through one o'clock. The sun was starting to bear down on Rob, and he was ready for a break. But he could also see that they were almost finished, and he realized that Mr. Larson only wanted to finish the job before they quit. So Rob didn't mind as much that they kept going. By 1:30 they had finished mowing and raking the field, and Mr. Larson never stopped his tractor until they were back at the barn. Mr. Larson stopped his tractor and swung on off and started back toward Rob. Rob shut his off and swung down too.

"You did a fine job, today, Rob. I couldn't have done any better myself."

"Thank you, Sir." The 'sir' just kind of popped out of Rob's mouth, and it surprised him.

"Our lunch is probably cold. How about we go into town and grab us a bite to eat?"

"Sounds great to me."

"Wash the dust off and meet me back at the truck in about ten minutes."

Rob went into the house and as he cleaned up, he couldn't help thinking how strange it was that he was excited about going into town to eat at a little rinky-dink cafe. Boy, how my priorities have changed, he thought. In California, going out to eat was an almost daily occurrence. His mother didn't usually have time to make dinner, so Rob would run out to get a hamburger three or four times a week. Then they would order pizza at least once a week. Rob hadn't had pizza since he had arrived in Montana. He didn't even think they had a pizza place in town.

He was back out to the truck in less than ten minutes, and Mr. Larson was out only a short time later. They both hopped in the truck and headed off toward town. Nowadays, when they came to the gate at the end of the drive, Rob didn't wait to be told. He hopped out and opened it, making sure he closed it and locked it after the truck had passed. The town was only about ten miles away, but it took about twenty minutes to get there because the first few miles of road were gravel; and the road all the way into town was narrow and winding. But to Rob it seemed like no time at all before they had pulled up in front of the small cafe. Mr. Larson parked his truck alongside several other pickups.

When they entered the cafe, Rob saw quite a few men who looked a lot like Mr. Larson– jeans, western shirt, cowboy hat and boots. It seemed that all eyes in the cafe were focused on them as they walked across the dining room floor. Most of the men nodded as they passed; several of them spoke a greeting to Mr. Larson. Rob and Mr. Larson slid into a booth facing the window front of the cafe. They had no more than gotten in their seats when a young man about Rob's age walked over to them. He had long, brown hair that came out from under his cowboy hat, at least longer than what Rob was used to seeing around here. He stopped in front of Mr. Larson, took off his hat and said, "Good afternoon, Mr. Larson."

Rob could tell that the boy was very uncomfortable. He was looking down and sort of fidgeting, waiting for Mr. Larson to acknowledge him. Rob saw someone not much unlike himself.

Mr. Larson looked at the boy for a moment and said, "Hello, Billy, what can I do for you?"

"I hear you're about to start balin' hay, and I was wonderin' if you could give me a job. I could use a little extra money at the moment."

Mr. Larson stared intently at the young man for a moment. Rob wondered what exactly was going on. He could sense that this was not a normal situation. He could sense the nervousness in the boy who stood before them. "We all could, Billy," Mr. Larson finally said. "Billy, if you work for me, you know it's on my terms, right? If I even think you've been drinking or anything else, you're gone; and you'll never work for me again and probably none of the other ranchers around here either. Do you understand that?"

"Yes sir, I do," Billy answered as he stood there fumbling with his hat in his hands. "Thank you, sir. I'll work hard."

"I know you will, Billy. Be at the house at 5:30 in the morning."

"I'll be there."

With that, Billy turned around and walked out of the cafe.

"What was that all about?" Rob asked.

"Well, you see, Billy's gotten himself a reputation as a troublemaker around here. Won't hardly anyone hire him to do any work anymore."

"Why'd you hire him then?" Rob asked.

"Well, I just think everybody needs another chance to redeem himself. In the Bible someone asks Jesus if he should forgive his brother seven times. Jesus tells him that he should forgive him seven times seventy, which to me means you should never give up on someone."

Mr. Larson was looking at Rob so intensely that he had to look away. He knew that Mr. Larson was talking about him, and he wanted to tell him thank you for all that he had done for him. But the words just wouldn't come out of his mouth. The waitress broke the silence when she walked up and asked, "What can I get for you men today?"

Rob couldn't help but think about how many people had called him a man since he had gotten to Montana. Funny, he thought, he didn't think of himself as a man at all. He hadn't ever really wanted to think of himself as a man because that required responsibility, and he hadn't ever wanted responsibility before. But lately he found that a certain pride came with responsibility, and he liked that feeling. He liked how he felt when he was given the responsibility, and he completed the job. He liked it when Mr. Larson told him he had done a good job. Maybe responsibility wasn't such a bad thing after all.

Chapter 10

When Rob came down the stairs at five a.m., Sylvia and Mary, Sylvia's friend, were already in the kitchen. Mr. Larson had said that he wanted to be in the field by six. It would already be light enough to work by that time, and the more they got done before the sun got well up in the sky, the cooler it would be. Even at this elevation, by noon it would be getting hot, especially out in the middle of a hay field where there is no shade at all. Mrs. Larson was already in the kitchen making breakfast. She smiled at Rob as he entered. "Good morning, sleepyhead. Pancakes alright with you this morning?"

"Sure," Rob replied. He walked over and poured himself a cup of coffee. He had never drunk coffee before he had arrived here, but it seemed so natural for him now to pour himself a cup. It was so pleasant in the cool morning to sit with a nice, hot cup of coffee in his hands.

Mrs. Larson turned to Rob and said, "Ron went outside to hook up the trailer to the truck."

Rob said, "I think I'll go see if I can give him a hand." As he walked out the door, he smiled thinking about how Mr. and

Mrs. Larson did things. Mrs. Larson didn't tell him to go out and help Mr. Larson. She didn't even ask him to go out and help. She only made the statement that he was out there. She left it up to Rob to decide if he should go out or not. It took Rob quite a while to figure out how the people around here did things. He found they never asked for help or said they needed it. They would always gladly accept your help; but if you didn't offer, they'd still get the job done. And they would never complain about it either. He thought about his friends back in California. If they needed to get something done, they paid somebody else to do it. And if they didn't have the money, the job usually didn't get done.

Mr. Larson was backing the truck up to the trailer when Rob got out there. He helped Mr. Larson lift the trailer up and set it down on the trailer hitch of the truck.

"Thanks, Rob. Looks like it's going to be a beautiful day. Are you ready to bale hay?"

"Why not? Since I've been here, I've shoveled horse manure, fed cows, driven a tractor. I might as well go for the full cowboy experience and bale hay." Rob said as he smiled at Mr. Larson.

"Don't go callin' yourself a cowboy yet. You haven't strung barbed wire, branded a cow, or ridden in a rodeo." Mr. Larson laughed and put his arm around Rob's shoulder as they started toward the house. As they walked along, a pair of headlights turned in the drive. "That must be Billy, and he's right on time," Mr. Larson said.

Mr. Larson and Rob walked over to meet Billy as he got out of his truck. "Morning Billy," Mr. Larson called. "Billy, this is my nephew, Rob. You didn't give me the chance to introduce you yesterday. He's going to be your partner today. He's never baled hay before, so you'll need to show him the ropes."

Billy and Rob said hello and shook hands, and the three of them went into the house. Mrs. Larson invited Billy to sit down and have breakfast with them. As Billy told her he'd love to join them, Mr. Larson was headed out the door. "I've already had my breakfast this morning, so I'm going to head on out and start baling. I'll get a good head start on you all, and, hopefully, you won't have to wait on me. Honey, make sure Rob has everything he needs. Why don't you folks try to get to the field by 6:30." Mrs. Larson gave him a quick kiss on the cheek and told him that they would be there soon.

By 6:15, they were all out in the hay field. Rob could see Mr. Larson out on the tractor, and there was already a circle around the field of small, square bales of hay. Mrs. Larson drove up beside the first bale. Sylvia and Mary jumped up on the trailer, and Billy started walking over to the bale. He turned to Rob and said, "It's real easy. All you do is throw the bales up to the girls and they stack them." He grabbed the bale and tossed it up on the trailer. It didn't seem to take any effort at all. Rob grabbed the next one and was surprised at the weight. He found himself struggling to get it up on the trailer. He thought he couldn't be that much weaker than Billy.

Then Billy walked up to him smiling and said, "Look, you're going to die if you try to pick those bales up like that all day. You don't lift them up there; you kind of swing them up. You use their momentum to get them up." Billy grabbed a bale, stepped forward, and swung it up. "See."

Rob grabbed the next bale and swung it up like Billy had shown him, and it went right up on the trailer. This went on for the next two hours until the trailer was completely full of hay. Mrs. Larson told Billy and Rob to hop in the truck. Then she drove over into the shade at the edge of the field where Mr. Larson was already resting.

The girls hopped off the back of the trailer. Everyone else got out of the truck, and they all walked over to where Mr. Larson was seated. "Well, at this pace, we should be finished by 4:00. That's a couple hours sooner than I expected. You folks are doing a real good job."

Rob and Billy sat down near Mr. Larson. Billy pulled out a pack of cigarettes from his pocket. He said to Mr. Larson, "Do you mind if I smoke?"

"Go right ahead, Billy. They're your lungs."

Billy noticed Rob eyeing the cigarettes, so he held out the pack toward Rob and asked, "Do you want one?"

Rob looked at the others around him and said, "No, man. I quit."

After a short break, they all got back to work. Rob had never worked so hard in his life. Just as Mr. Larson had predicted, they were finished by a short time after 4:00. Rob was never so glad to have finished anything. He felt as though his arms would soon fall off, and his back was so sore that he knew he would have trouble getting out of bed tomorrow. Rob had enjoyed working alongside Billy. Billy had been a lot of fun. He didn't seem like such a bad person at all to Rob. Why did he have such a bad reputation? But then Rob thought about how he had a bad reputation back home, and he didn't think of himself as a bad person, either.

Billy had driven his truck out to the field, so Rob, Sylvia, and Mary all jumped in the truck and rode back to the ranch with Billy. As they pulled into the drive, Billy turned to Rob and said, "What're you doin' tonight? There's a lake nearby where people gather to party. You want to ride along?" Sylvia gave Rob a look that told him that she didn't approve at all, so he said, "Not tonight, Billy. Maybe some other time I can."

Sylvia looked at Rob and said, "Well, if you want to go back to partying and being a jerk, tonight's as good a night as any."

"Hey, Sylvia, that's not what I meant. I'm through with partying. I only meant that I'd like to visit with him again. I haven't met any other guys my age since I moved here. I'm just glad I finally met somebody cool around here. I mean, I have been going nuts around this place."

"I didn't realize I was such bad company," Sylvia said.

Rob sensed the aggravation in her voice and quickly said, "I didn't mean it that way, Sylvia. It's just nice to get to speak to another guy."

They pulled up in front of the ranch house, and Rob was relieved to be able to get out of that situation. He knew Sylvia was mad at him, and he didn't want her upset. He hopped out of the truck and walked around to Billy's side. He extended his hand and said, "I'm really glad to meet you, Billy."

"Nice meeting you too, Rob," Billy smiled as he shook Rob's hand.

Rob felt Billy slide something into the palm of his hand.

"Yeah, it was really nice to meet you too."

Rob thought, Oh, man, a cigarette. It's been nearly three weeks. I can't wait to get out behind the barn and smoke this thing. If only it were something else. No, I can't think that way. I've got to stay straight.

Billy waved as he got in his truck and drove away.

"He's a really cool guy," Rob said to Sylvia as they walked toward the house.

"He's not the type of person you should hang around, Rob. He's always getting into trouble."

"What kind of trouble is there to get into around here?" Rob asked. "What's he done? Let somebody's sheep out of their pen."

"There are lots of nice guys around here, Rob. Why is it that the first time you meet someone who's a known trouble-maker, you think you've found a friend?" Sylvia started to walk away quickly, and Rob could tell that she was mad at him.

"Hey, all I said was that he was a cool guy. I didn't say that I was going to start hanging out with him. You act as though we're going to go start robbing gas stations together."

Sylvia stopped and turned to face him. She could hardly control the anger welling up inside of her. "Well, I really thought you were changing. I really thought you wanted to be a better person. And the minute someone shows up who's like the people you used to hang out with, you go right back to being the same old Rob."

"Hey, Sylvia, believe me. I am not the same old Rob. The old Rob would have ridden off with Billy to go party with him, and you probably wouldn't have seen me for a couple of days. Trust me, Sylvia. I'm trying to do better."

Sylvia looked down and smiled slightly. "Yeah, you're right, Rob. You have changed. Do you know I enjoy your company now? When you got here, I wanted Dad to send you away somewhere. I thought you'd never change."

"Well, I have, Sylvia. And I enjoy your company too."

They turned and walked quietly into the house. Both of them felt a little awkward, and neither of them had anything else to say.

All through dinner all Rob could think about was that cigarette in his pocket. He could hardly keep from grinning. 'Dinner and a smoke,' he thought. What could be better? As soon as he had finished dinner and helped with the dishes, he casually mentioned that he thought he'd walk out and get some fresh air.

As he walked out toward the barn, he began to realize how much he did enjoy the fresh air. He breathed deeply as he walked along. The cool evening air made the scent of the evergreens crisper. He felt more alive than he had felt in years. The air was invigorating to him. It occurred to him that his sense of smell had improved since he had quit smoking, even though it was involuntarily. He couldn't remember how long it had been since he'd been this happy. The moon was rising behind him, and he could actually look out and make out the details of the mountains. He could see the tree line and even make out individual trees. He could see a little snow that still hadn't melted up near the peaks. He stopped for a moment and took in the beauty around him. For a moment, a brief moment, he thought about tearing up the cigarette. Then he thought, ah, it's just one.

He now loved the smell of the barn. The blend of horses and hay brought an earthy scent to his nostrils. The moon was so bright outside that he could look around inside the barn without even turning on the lights. Suddenly, the realization hit him that he actually liked living here. If friends back in California had told him that he would have liked living on a ranch, he would have told them that they were crazy. He walked over and lingered around Golden Boy's stall for a moment. The horse came up and nuzzled at his hand when he stuck it out toward him.

"Hey, boy. It's not long till your big day, is it? I know you guys are going to do just fine." He gently rubbed the horse behind its ears. Golden Boy always responded when someone did that. He moved his head up and down and pressed it against Rob's hand. Rob put his arm around the horse's neck and put his cheek up against it.

"Yeah, you're a good horse."

Then he walked over and grabbed the chair that Sylvia used when she cleaned and polished the horses' hooves. He sat down right by Rising Star's stall, pulled out his cigarette, leaned back in the chair and said aloud, "Yeah, this isn't a bad life. One more smoke and then I'll call it quits. How about it, Rising Star? Should I quit? Yeah, I think so too. Now I think I'll just enjoy this last smoke."

He leaned back in the chair, lit the cigarette, tilted his head back and took a deep drag. He didn't say anything else while he finished the cigarette. When he had smoked it on down, he thumped the butt out the door of the barn, stood up, and said, "Well, I guess I'll see you guys bright and early in the morning." He patted Golden Boy on the neck one more time and walked out of the barn and back to the house. He took out a piece of gum and popped it in his mouth so that Sylvia wouldn't have any idea he'd had a cigarette.

As he walked back toward the house, he thought once again about how much his life had changed in the last few months and how much he enjoyed the ranch. As he neared the house, he stopped and took one more deep breath of the cool, crisp mountain air before he stepped inside. Smoke! He smelled smoke. He turned in a panic and saw flames leaping up the side of the barn. He opened the front door and screamed, "Fire! The barn's on fire."

The whole family had been sitting together in the living room. Everyone jumped up and started running toward the door. Mr. Larson grabbed his wife's shoulder and said, "Call the Fire Department." When he first exited the front door, he could already see that they were too late. Sylvia was out in front of him, and he could hear her screaming, crying. He knew that he had to catch her, or she would run right into that barn after her horses.

Rob was out in front of all of them screaming, "NO! NO! NO!" He could hear the horses' shrieks of terror and pain. Luckily, only two of the horses were in the stable, the two they were taking to the coming weekend's competition. Sadly, though, they were Sylvia's favorites, Rising Star and Golden Boy.

By the time Rob reached the barn, flames were everywhere, leaping up the sides and into the hayloft. Rising Star and Golden Boy were going crazy. Rob could hear them kicking and thrashing about. As he started to pull open the doors to the barn, Sylvia was beside him. Opening the barn doors only ignited the flames more, and an intense wave of heat rushed over them. Embers cascaded down around them. The crackling and popping wood sounded like firecrackers. Even though it had only been a matter of minutes, pieces of timber from the loft were already splitting and falling to the floor below.

For a moment Rob thought, 'What am I doing? It's total chaos in here.' But he ran on in beside Sylvia, and as she opened Golden Boy's stall, he opened Rising Star's. Rob expected the horse to bolt out when he opened the stall, but Rising Star was rearing, kicking about, and not about to leave her stall. He looked over and saw Sylvia grabbing the other horse's halter to try to lead him out. Suddenly, there was a loud crack and a large flaming plank came crashing down into Golden Boy's stall hitting the horse right across the back. The horse jumped back, pulling Sylvia off her feet. Rob panicked but was quickly relieved to see Sylvia jump back to her feet. She grabbed the horse's halter again and started to lead the animal out. The next thing Rob knew Mr. Larson was in the stall beside him, and he quickly had a hold of Rising Star's halter.

"Come on, Rob. Let's get out of here before this thing collapses." Mr. Larson began pulling the horse out of the stall, but the horse was fighting him desperately. Then Rob saw that Sylvia was having a hard time with Golden Boy who seemed determined to stay in his stall. Rob ran over and grabbed hold of the halter as well. Flames now filled the loft above them, sending sparks throughout the barn. Rob suddenly realized his clothes were being burned by embers as he struggled with the horse. Sylvia was screaming and pulling at the horse's halter. Then Rob remembered a movie he had seen when he was young where they tied something over a horse's eyes to lead it out of a burning barn, so he pulled off his jacket and threw it over the horse's head. At first the horse jumped back even more violently, but then it seemed to calm slightly; and they quickly led the animal out of the barn.

When they were finally out of the stable, Mr. Larson called to them and said, "Let's take them all the way up to the house and get them completely away from the fire. Lily, call the vet. Tell him to get out here as quickly as possible."

Rob walked alongside Golden Boy as Sylvia led him toward the house, and he could smell the singed hair and flesh of the horse. He glanced back at the barn behind them, and he couldn't believe they had just been inside of the inferno he now witnessed. Flames leapt toward the sky and illuminated the night.

Rob didn't know what to say to Sylvia. He knew that she was crying, but what could he say. They led the horse up to where Mr. Larson was already examining Rising Star. Rob started to look closely at Golden Boy for the first time. Up to now he had only been concerned with getting the horse away from the fire. He immediately saw a big gash across the horse's back where the large timber had come crashing down. The torn and burned flesh made him recoil and look away. Sylvia had her arms around the horse's neck and was trying her best to keep him calm. Her sobbing told him that she had already seen the injury.

Mr. Larson came over to examine Golden Boy. "How's Rising Star?" Rob asked.

Mr. Larson looked at Rob for a moment before he spoke. "Well, she's not hurt as badly as Golden Boy, but she has several burns that are going to have to be treated. Also, we don't know if the fire has damaged their lungs. That's my greatest fear. I only hope we got them out of there quickly enough."

Mr. Larson continued to stare at Rob, and Rob couldn't face his him. He had to turn his head away from Mr. Larson.

Finally, Mr. Larson said. "Rob, I have to ask you. Do you know anything about the fire?"

Two months ago, Rob would have lied. Even though he would have known, just as now, that Mr. Larson knew that he had something to do with the fire, he still would have lied. Now he found that he had to tell the truth. His emotions were welling up inside of him. "Yes sir. But I didn't mean for it to happen at all. I'm so sorry. Billy had given me a cigarette, and I went out to the barn to smoke it. The hay must have caught fire when I threw the cigarette away. I'm so sorry."

Mr. Larson didn't reply. He walked over to look at Rising Star and started to talk to the horse. Rob now heard the sirens in the distance, but it was way too late. The barn was already beginning to crumble, a burning shell now. Rob didn't know what to do. He wanted to run, but there was nowhere to go, nowhere to hide.

As the fire truck turned into the drive, Mr. Larson walked out to meet them. Rob decided to walk on into the house and up to his room. He couldn't face Mr. Larson or Sylvia, and there was nothing that could be done about the barn. So the only thing left for him to do was to pack his bags, for he knew that they would be sending him away tomorrow.

Chapter 11

Several days passed, and Rob had not been sent away. Actually, hardly a word had been said to him. The house was silent around him. They ate their meals in silence. They did their chores in silence. It was almost as if he weren't there. No one said anything to him, not even Grandfather. He noticed, though, that everyone seemed to get quiet when he entered the room. He thought to himself that they must be still discussing what to do. But he knew it was only a matter of time. They would send him away, and why shouldn't they? He was nothing but trouble.

The veterinarian had given them some medication for the horses that had to be applied several times a day. He also said that the horses couldn't be ridden for quite some time. Rob had expected that. And the rodeo was only three days away. Sylvia only came out of her room to go care for the horses, and then she would return. She hadn't said a single word to Rob since the fire. Rob couldn't stand the silent treatment any longer. He had to talk to her. Even though he could hardly face her, he had to tell her how badly he felt.

Rob knew she was ignoring him, but he had to see her. He knocked on her door and gently called, "Sylvia."

After more than a minute of standing by her door calling, he slowly opened it. He knew she was in there, so he said, "Sylvia, I really want to talk to you."

When he had pushed the door open far enough, he could see her lying on the bed. "Sylvia, please talk to me."

She turned toward him and said as hatefully as she could, "Get out of my room. I never want to see you again."

"Please, Sylvia, I want to tell you how sorry I am."

"You are always telling us how sorry you are," she said vehemently. "You think you can do whatever you want, hurt whoever you want; and you can say you're sorry and they should forgive you. Well, it doesn't work that way. I tried, but I just can't do it anymore. If you really meant it when you said you were sorry, you'd try to change. You'd try to quit hurting people. But you haven't. You'll never change."

Rob desperately wanted her to understand that he had changed. Couldn't she see that? "Please, Sylvia, I didn't mean it. I wish that I could go back and change that moment. I wish more than you'll ever know that it hadn't happened. Can't you understand that? Please let me make it up to you."

"Get out of my room," Sylvia said one last time. Then she turned her head away and buried her face in her pillow. Rob stood there in the door for a moment longer and finally turned and walked back out of her room. He had never felt this badly in his life. Why? Why did he have to go out to the barn with that cigarette? Why did he have to meet Billy? He had finally begun to care for someone, and he had blown it. What could he do to make it up to her?

He went back into his room and lay down across his bed. All he could think was why. Why was he always screwing up his life? Why did he always have to hurt other people? He had been trying. He really had, but now he had blown it again. He couldn't blame Sylvia for not liking him. Her horses meant a lot to her. And she had looked forward all summer long to competing in this rodeo, here in front of her hometown. Now he had ruined it for her. Yes, he couldn't blame her.

...

The next morning before anyone else got up Rob walked out to the small aspen grove he had discovered a few weeks earlier. Grandfather had talked to him about finding a place where he could find himself. This was his place. A small outcropping of rock near the edge of the grove formed a perfect place to sit. From this perch he could see down to the ranch below. The pastures spread out before him, the horses grazed over the green grass, the dew sparkled in the morning light.

In the few short weeks since he had discovered this oasis he had come here often. It always cleared his mind to sit here in the aspen grove. It was so peaceful, so serene. But now his mind was racing; tears were in his eyes. All he could think was Why? Why did he have to be so stupid? Things had been going so well. But now he knew they would send him away. He couldn't blame them. Why would they let him stay?

Maybe he should just run away, he thought. No; one thing he had learned was that you can't run from trouble; you must face it. Yes, he would be sent back, and it would be a violation of his parole; but he would face it. He would take the punishment and become a better man because of it. He buried his face in his hands and wept: WHY?

The hand on his shoulder startled him so badly he nearly fell off the rock. He looked behind him and there stood Grandfather.

"Where did you come from? How did you get here? How'd you know I was here? I didn't hear you at all."

"So many questions; all of them pointless, and I thought you were learning." As Grandfather smiled at him, the sight of the old man that he had grown to love caused all his emotions to well up inside of him again. He buried his head into the old Indian's shoulder. Grandfather put his arms around the boy who was larger than he and didn't say anything for a long time.

Finally, the old man whispered, "So you've found your spot."

Rob looked up and gave him that look as he had so many times which seemed to say, "How did you know?" But the old man ignored it and said, "This is a good spot. You have chosen well."

"Yeah," Rob said, "I thought I would enjoy it one last time."

"Are you leaving?"

When Rob looked up, the old man was still smiling at him.

"Are you in such a hurry to leave us?"

"No, but there is no way they are going to let me stay now. Sylvia hates me."

The old man spread a blanket out on the ground. Then he sat down cross-legged and motioned for Rob to sit across from him, and he began to speak. "There was once a young Indian who was not yet a warrior, and he wanted to do something that would make everyone in the tribe know who he was. The game had disappeared from the area that his tribe called home, and they were in search of a new land. The young boy thought, 'If I can find much game and a new land, everyone will praise me and call me a man.' So he rose before the sun and sneaked out of the village. He took his pony and headed toward the mountains. This was the destination of his village. They knew they would find water there; and where there is water, they would find game. In his mind he pictured riding off to the mountains and finding a beautiful valley full of game. He would return that evening and tell them all what he had found, and everyone in the village would be calling his name. They would be talking for many years about how he had found their new homeland. His chest swelled as he thought of this.

He rode on through the morning thinking of all the good things others would say of him. He had a very pleasant morning as he rode along, his thoughts on only himself. It was not until the early afternoon that the realization struck him that he had been riding for nearly half the day and the mountains still seemed a great distance away. This realization struck him like a cold wind. There was no way that he could even reach the mountains today, let alone find his beautiful valley and return home a hero. It would be hard for him to even make it home before dark. If he did not make it home by dark, his family would worry. He had told no one of his plan. Even now his family was probably wondering where he was. They would not be worried yet, for he often went exploring with his friends or alone, but he had never returned home after dark.

The warriors of the tribe would probably set out looking for him if he had not returned by evening. The whole village would know he was missing. Instead of being a hero, he now realized he would be shamed. The elders would lecture him for his foolishness. So in less than an hour he had gone from thinking that he would be a hero to realizing that he had been a fool."

Rob sat silently with his head bowed, listening to the old man speak.

"Tell me, Rob, what are you thinking?"

Rob never looked up but spoke to the old man with his eyes cast downward. "That the boy was a fool. He should have known that he couldn't help the tribe."

"Ah, but the boy rode on toward home, feeling much as you do now. He felt that he could no longer be a part of the tribe. They would never accept him again. He didn't even want to return, but he knew that the warriors would continue to search for him and waste valuable time, time they should spend searching for game. So he decided that he would return home and then tell them that he would become an outcast, forced to live out on his own or to find a tribe that would accept him. But who would want him, he thought, as he slowly made his way back toward the tribe, accepting the fact that this would be his last night with them.

He followed the creek that led to his tribe's encampment. Dusk settled around him. In another forty-five minutes it would be dark. He knew, though, that he was no more than an hour's ride from camp. The horse meandered along. He let the horse follow its own lead. He had been traveling for about another twenty minutes when he noticed the horse's ears come up. He immediately became alert. Something had alarmed the horse, and he sensed that something was not right. He halted the horse and strained his eyes and ears for any sound or sight. He remained perfectly still.

Then he saw it. Something moved about 100 yards ahead of him. He slipped quietly off the horse and tied the animal to a tree. He began to slowly move forward, making no sound whatsoever. He had been taught well by his father and was known as an excellent hunter, even for his age. He moved quietly along the creek. He would proceed forward about 10 yards and then wait silently to try to detect any movement. He was no more than 30 yards away when he saw them.

And he silently blessed his Keeper as he realized how lucky he had been that he had not been detected. For there, camped that short distance away was a group of Pawnee warriors. His heart was pounding so loudly that he was afraid they would hear it. He stood there for a moment trying to compose himself and to decide what he must do. After his breathing and his heart had calmed a little, he began to make his way back toward his pony. He could not believe his good fortune. If he had ridden only a short distance farther, he was sure that he would now be dead. He must return to his camp and warn the others.

After untying the pony, he began backtracking so that he could make a wide circle around the Pawnee. In less than thirty minutes he saw the fires of his own camp. He could see the men of the camp all gathered together. He knew that he was probably the reason for this gathering. When they saw him, they all began to run toward him. He could see the anger on their faces. But before they could speak, he breathlessly called out, 'Pawnee.' The demeanor of the crowd changed instantly. Questions began to fly at him. One of the elders of the tribe raised his hand for silence, helped the young Brave down off his horse, and said, 'Come, you must tell us about the Pawnee.'

He led the boy into a nearby teepee. Several of the elders and some of the braves followed him.

'Now tell us what you know.'

The young boy was still shaking from running into the Pawnee, but he tried his best to control his emotions as he spoke. He was thinking that, luckily, they had not yet asked him where he had been. 'As I was returning to our camp, I was following along the stream when I saw movement up ahead of me. I crept closer for a better look, and I saw a group of Pawnee warriors camped along the stream bank. Their faces were painted for war, and they were camped without a fire.'

'Where were they camped?' the old warrior asked.

'Down around the bend with the high cliff.' The young boy was now glad that he had explored so much with his friends because he was able to let the warriors know exactly how far away the Pawnee were.

The old Indian turned immediately to the others in the teepee. 'Gather the tribal leaders. We must discuss this matter now.'

As the others left the teepee, the old Indian turned back to the boy. 'Now tell me all that you know.' The boy then continued to tell the elder all that he had seen. After much discussion, the council decided to move the tribe out that night and to slip away from the Pawnee. The Pawnee had planned to attack the village at daylight, but all they would find were smoldering fires. The boy became a hero among his friends, and he was never chastised for causing his family much grief over his disappearance. Later, the boy would become a respected leader in his tribe. That day he had learned the value of not acting rashly and of thinking about his actions before he did them."

The old man sat quietly staring at Rob after he had finished his story. "Now why have I told you this?"

Rob looked up suddenly at the man he called Grandfather. Rob always suspected that all of the old Indian's stories were supposed to be teaching him some type of lesson, but never before had he asked Rob for an explanation.

The old Indian saw the puzzled look on Rob's face, smiled and said, "What did you learn?"

Rob was still confused. "I didn't learn anything. Is this young boy supposed to be me? Our stories are nothing alike. Sure, he did something stupid, but then he became a hero. I just did something stupid."

Grandfather smiled at the young man beside him. "Well, now you must do something that will give you honor. Think, what problem do you now face?"

"Well, everyone hates me. That's a problem." Tears started to well up in Rob's eyes again. He looked away, for he could no longer face the man who had taught him so much. "I burned down Mr. Larson's barn, and I caused Sylvia to not be able to ride in the rodeo. There's nothing I can do to change things." Rob slumped over and buried his head in his arms.

Grandfather leaned over and put his arm around Rob's shoulders. "My young son, there are always things you can do. Never are things hopeless. You just have to speak to the spirits and ask for guidance, and they will show you the way. The wind will whisper the answer to you when you think there is none. The trees will call out to you when you think all is lost. All you have to do is to have faith and listen to them speaking to you. Now let's ask the Great Spirit and listen for his answer."

Rob put his arms around the old man and said, "Why, why haven't you given up on me? Why are you so nice to me? You of all people should hate me."

"And why is that my young friend?" The old Indian was now facing Rob.

"Well, because of why I am here, of course."

"And do you know why are you here?"

Rob looked up at the old man. "You know why I am here."

Grandfather looked solemnly at Rob and said, "Yes, I do know why you are here. But my question was do you know why you are here?"

Rob found himself getting a little angry and impatient with the old man, and he said, "Of course, for getting in that fight down at the beach."

Grandfather stared intently at Rob. "So that is what you think? Tell me, why did you go down to the beach to attack the young man?"

Rob looked at Grandfather. "What do you mean? We didn't go down there to attack him. It just happened."

Grandfather leaned over toward Rob and lowered his voice, even softer than he normally spoke, as if he were telling Rob a secret. "Nothing just happens. Everything is for a reason. We are talking now for a reason. There is a purpose to all our actions. To become a man, you must learn to look for the purpose. You must learn to ask, why did this happen? And you must listen to the Spirit for the answer. That is why we are here now. We must listen and find the answer. Now we must sit quietly and listen to what the Spirit tells us. Then we shall see what must be done."

The old man bowed his head and began to quietly chant. Rob bowed his own head and began to listen to the chant of the old Indian. He soon found himself drifting, and he began to quietly chant along. And there they remained as the sun slowly drifted across the sky.

Chapter 12

Rob walked into the living room where Mr. Larson sat looking over his books. He walked up to the desk and said, "Mr. Larson, may I speak with you?"

Mr. Larson looked up from his work and saw immediately that Rob had something serious to discuss with him. He had been waiting for this moment, hoping it would come. "Would you like to go in to the study, Rob?"

"Yes sir."

Mr. Larson walked into the study, around the large oak desk, and sat down. He motioned for Rob to pull up a seat. "So, what's on your mind?"

Rob took a deep breath and thought about what he had to say. Finally, he looked Mr. Larson in the eye and said, "I know that you are probably wanting to send me back to California right now, and I really can't blame you. I know what I did has cost you and your family a lot of money. And not only that, I destroyed whatever trust you folks were starting to have in me." Then Rob looked down. "And I hurt Sylvia most of all. I have been trying to think of how I could repay you for all that you have done for me and for everything I have destroyed; if you'll just give me the chance, I think I have an idea about how to make everything up to all of you."

Mr. Larson looked at Rob long and hard. Rob continued to look at Mr. Larson. There was a time in the past when Rob could not have continued to look into those piercing eyes, a time when he was usually trying to hide something from others, and he would have looked away. Now he had nothing to hide. He knew what he was doing was the right thing, and he felt a sense of pride in what he had to say. He knew he had done something very wrong, and now he wanted to do something to make amends for what he had done. Then Mr. Larson said, "Well, tell me what you have in mind."

"Mr. Larson," Rob began, "I destroyed your barn. Whether I meant to or not, I did. And I destroyed Sylvia's chance to ride Golden Boy in the rodeo. I know that she won't be able to ride Golden Boy, but I might have a way she can still participate in the rodeo. Mr. Larson, you've always paid me for the times I've helped you work around the ranch. Now I want to work for you while you rebuild your barn, but I don't want to get paid for it. It's only right that I help you."

Mr. Larson started to speak, but Rob interrupted him by putting up his hand and said, "Wait, Mr. Larson. Hear me out first if you would. Let me tell you everything I have in mind. Sylvia had told me that Billy has what was once considered one of the best barrel racing horses in the county. Ya know, Billy needs a job really badly, and he said he's done quite a bit of carpentry work. What if you tell Billy that you'll hire him to help rebuild the barn if he would be willing to kind of rent out his horse to us for Sylvia to ride? He'd have a job, and he'd get some extra money for letting Sylvia ride his horse."

Again Mr. Larson began to speak and again Rob held up his hand and said, "Please let me finish before you speak. Just give me a chance." There was a pleading in his voice.

Mr. Larson nodded and said, "Go ahead, Rob."

"Well, here's how I got it figured. I've saved up nearly four hundred dollars this summer. I would offer Billy the four hundred to let Sylvia ride his horse, and then you could pay Billy the money that you normally pay me to work around here. I would help for free. I don't know that much about carpentry, but I would do the best I could; and I would do everything you asked of me." Rob now looked down waiting for Mr. Larson to reply. He stood there humbly, quietly, patiently.

Mr. Larson thought for a few moments, pondering, before he responded. "Rob, I think that's a good plan, but I do have a couple of questions. First, do you think Billy would rent out his horse? And, more importantly, do you think we can count on Billy?"

"I think, Mr. Larson, that sometimes you just got to trust someone and hope that they'll do the right thing."

Mr. Larson stood up, smiled, put his hand on Rob's shoulder and said, "Yeah, I think you're right about that, Rob. Come on. Let's you and me ride into town and see if we can find Billy and have a talk with him."

"Well, should we ask Sylvia what she would think about riding Billy's horse before we talk to him?" Rob asked.

"I think we ought to keep this to ourselves for the time being," Mr. Larson replied. "Let's go on into town."

Chapter 13

❀

Rob and Mr. Larson got back to the ranch just before dinnertime. Rob could hardly contain his excitement as they entered the house. Billy had agreed to everything, and he was even excited about the plan. He had wanted to get involved with the rodeo again, had wanted someone to ride his horse; but he didn't know how to go about it. And he was excited about working around the ranch. It seemed that Rob's plan had pleased everyone, at least everyone so far.

Mr. Larson told Rob to wait until dinner to tell Sylvia so that everyone in the family would hear about his plan. Rob was so excited he thought they'd never all get seated at the dinner table. Finally, after everyone one began to eat, Mr. Larson nodded at Rob. He cleared his throat and began to speak.

"Sylvia?" When Sylvia looked up at him, he could still see the loathing in her eyes. He almost didn't have the courage to go on, but he knew he must. "You are going to be able to ride in the rodeo this weekend."

"What?" Sylvia said incredulously. "What are you talking about?"

Rob hesitated before speaking up again. "I've figured out a way for you to ride in the rodeo. It's all arranged."

"What?" Sylvia said again more forcefully than before, looking at him in disbelief.

"Yes, you are going to be able to ride in the rodeo. I've made a deal with Billy, and he's going to let you ride his horse."

"What?" Sylvia said a third time, rising from her seat as she did so. To Rob's surprise Sylvia seemed even more angry. He thought she'd be as excited as he was. Even though he felt like shutting up and leaving the room, he continued.

"Billy is willing to let you ride his horse in the rodeo. You said yourself that it was one of the best horses on the circuit. And Billy said he's actually been training it, and it's in good shape and ready to run. He thinks you could win this thing."

"You just don't understand, do you?" Sylvia said. "This rodeo was not about me riding; it was about me showing off my horse. I've raised that horse since it was born. I broke it, trained it. I entered this rodeo as a sort of coming of age party for my horse. I wanted to prove to everyone that he was the best horse in the county. I'm not going to ride Billy's horse in that rodeo, or any other old hag you can find."

Then Sylvia turned and fled the room. Everyone just sat at the table and looked after her. No one spoke; no one got up; no one even moved. Rob was heartbroken. He had done everything he could think of to make it right with Sylvia, and he had failed. Finally, Mr. Larson said, "Let me speak to her. I'll be right back."

"Sylvia?" Mr. Larson called from the door as he opened it slightly.

"Just go away. I don't want to talk right now," Sylvia answered.

"No," Mr. Larson replied. "We do need to talk right now."

He entered the room and sat down on the edge of the bed where Sylvia was now lying.

"Sylvia, you do need to ride in this rodeo," he began.

"But I just can't, Dad. I can't. I've had my heart set on riding Golden Boy for as long as I can remember. I just couldn't ride any other horse right now."

"But don't you see, Sylvia, you need to ride this horse because it's the right thing to do. It's the right thing to do for Billy. And it's the right thing to do for Rob."

"I don't care if it's the right thing to do for them. I don't care if it's the right thing to do for anyone. I just want to do what's the right thing to do for me right now."

"But little girl," Mr. Larson put his hand on Sylvia's shoulder as he spoke, and Sylvia thought that she couldn't remember the last time he called her little girl, "sometimes you have to think of others even when you don't want to. I know you are hurt right now, and I know how badly you wanted to ride your horse. But I think this would do more for Rob and Billy than you could ever imagine if you were to ride this horse. Plus," he smiled, "I think it would help you to get out there and ride that horse into the dust." Then Mr. Larson got up and walked toward the door, turned, and said, "Why don't you think about it for a little while then come tell me what you've decided." And with that he left the room.

...

The next morning when Sylvia came down to breakfast, everyone at the table stared at her, not knowing what to say or what she would say. She walked up to the table and stood there for a moment. Finally, she said: "Alright, I'll ride the horse."

"Yes!" Rob shouted, for he could hardly contain his excitement. "Okay, what do we need to do now?" he said to no one in particular.

"Well," Mr. Larson spoke up, "the rodeo is in only two days. We should go over to Billy's and get that horse over here so Sylvia can start practicing on him. She's been riding all the time, but every horse is a little different; she needs to run that horse through the ropes and get used to him. Sylvia, you start prepping the arena, and Rob and I will take the trailer and get that horse back here. You ought to wet it down a little and get the dust to settle. We'll be back shortly." With that, Rob and Mr. Larson were heading toward the door.

"But," Mrs. Larson protested, "you haven't even finished your breakfast. That horse can wait."

"No," Mr. Larson replied, "breakfast can wait. We've got work to do and only two days to get it done."

...

In less than two hours, Rob and Mr. Larson were pulling up to the ranch with the horse in tow. Billy was following right behind them in his truck. In no time the horse was unloaded and in the arena. Everyone was excited; anticipation hung in the air. Tomorrow they would take the horse to the rodeo grounds, so

Sylvia only had one day to work the horse and decide how she would ride him.

Everyone was excited, that is, but Sylvia. She seemed to only be going through the motions. Mr. Larson could tell that Billy had spent a lot of time lately training his horse. The animal was definitely in prime condition. If anything, Sylvia was slowing the horse down, and everyone around the arena knew it, everyone but Rob. But even he sensed that something wasn't right. As the morning wore on, the excitement wore off. Rob sensed a tension building, but he didn't know why. He thought that maybe they were all just worried that there wasn't enough time to prepare, that they just couldn't do it. Grandfather had walked off earlier and had seemed to be disappointed about something. Maybe, Rob thought, the horse isn't as good as Billy had said. Maybe it was useless. Finally, after Sylvia made one more run through the course, Billy jumped off the fence, walked out into the arena toward Sylvia, and said, "Let's forget it. I don't want you riding my horse anymore. Get off and take your saddle off him. We're going home."

"What?" Rob yelled as he started toward the center too. "What's going on? What do you mean, Billy?"

"Fine," Sylvia said as she jumped off the horse.

Mr. Larson now joined them in the center of the area.

"What's going on?" Rob asked again, looking from person to person, waiting for someone to respond.

"Well, it seems to me," Mr. Larson answered, "that Billy is upset because Sylvia isn't trying."

"That's right," Billy replied. "I don't want someone just out there taking my horse for a pleasure ride in the park. If he's going to run in this thing, I want someone who will try to win with him," he said looking directly at Sylvia.

"Well, I didn't want to ride your horse anyway," Sylvia said. "I was only doing this for you."

"You wouldn't be doing me any favors going out and not even trying with my horse. Anyone could take him out there and lose. I want everyone to see that he can win."

"That's what I wanted with my horse too," Sylvia replied almost in tears.

Billy walked up and faced Sylvia. "I know Rascal's not Golden Boy, but I think he's the best horse anywhere around, except for yours of course," he said jokingly. "Your horse is young, and I'm sure he's going to come through this fine. He has plenty of years of racing left in him. To tell you the truth, I really think he's too young to be racing anyway. In another year Golden Boy will be all the stronger and he'll be able to take the strain of racing a lot better. He's too young to be competing at the top level. He hasn't even run in any events yet, and you would have been taking him into one of the toughest competitions around."

"You know I agree with Billy on this one, Sylvia," Mr. Larson smiled and put his arm around her. "I've told you the same thing myself. There's nothing wrong with you going out and riding this horse and giving it everything you've got. You may have wanted to prove to everyone that you had the best horse, but I wouldn't mind you proving to everyone that my daughter is the best rider.

"But it just won't be the same," Sylvia replied.

"Nobody said it would be. But that doesn't mean you can't go out and do your best." "Okay," Sylvia said. "Let's do this thing. I don't have it in me to not try to win anyway."

Then they worked through the rest of the morning with a renewed enthusiasm. Rob immediately noticed a difference in Sylvia's performance. He now realized how obvious it would have been to everyone else that Sylvia had not been trying before. Now she seemed to be flying around the course with a vengeance. Billy and Mr. Larson were cheering her on. It was then that Rob noticed that Grandfather was back and standing beside him.

"So, Sylvia is riding now I see," Grandfather said.

There was a time when Rob wouldn't have understood and would've made some stupid comment about how she had been riding all day, but now he just smiled and nodded his head.

"But she still has far to go," Grandfather continued.

"She looks pretty good to me," Rob replied.

"No," Grandfather said turning to face Rob. "I speak of the anger she has inside. I had hoped that riding would ease her pain, but it has not."

"Maybe winning the rodeo will help her," Rob said.

"I think not, Rob. She will still believe that she could have done better on her horse."

Rob looked down and started to feel that it was useless, that he would never gain her trust and respect.

"Don't lose hope, my son," Grandfather said as he placed his hand on Rob's shoulder. "She will learn that you are becoming a new person and then she too will change."

"I think I am a new person, Grandfather," Rob said looking up at the old man.

"You are, my son, you are. But the key is to become a new person every day, become a better person every day. You have learned much in a very short time. But there is always more to learn. Have faith and let the Spirit guide you.

...

The next morning they were all up earlier than usual, and there was a sense of excitement in the kitchen. They wanted to have the horse at the rodeo grounds by eight o'clock, which meant they needed to leave by seven o'clock. They had loaded the saddle and gear in the trailer the night before. Everything was packed except the horse.

Rob rose early. He had hardly slept through the night thinking of the day's events ahead. When he went downstairs, he found the household was already bustling with activity.

"Good morning," Mrs. Larson called as he entered the kitchen.

Sylvia was pacing about the room. Finally, her mother walked over to her, put her arm around her shoulders and said, "Hey, calm down a little. Everything's going to be fine."

Sylvia kind of shrugged and said, "Yeah, I guess."

Rob had never been into athletics, but he had always heard about the benefits of a positive attitude; so Sylvia's attitude worried him. He wanted more than anything for Sylvia to win her barrel-racing event. He thought it would mean more to him that it would to her. Maybe then she would forgive him, he thought.

Soon, there was a knock on the door and Mr. Larson let Billy into the house. "Well, are we ready to go win us a rodeo?" he called as he entered the kitchen. He shook Rob's hand and said, "Let's go get that horse in the trailer. I'm ready to get on the road."

"Mind if I at least get something to eat first?" Rob replied, smiling.

"Well, as long as you don't take too long. Man, I'm so excited I could hardly sleep."

"Me too," Rob replied. Well, at least someone is excited, Rob thought. Maybe our excitement will become contagious. He looked over at Sylvia who was still pacing about. He wanted to say something to her, but he had no idea even where to begin.

After breakfast they all headed out to load the horse in the trailer. Even Grandfather went outside and helped. Everyone seemed to be excited about the upcoming event, everyone but Sylvia.

In no time they had the horse loaded onto the trailer, and Rob was on his way to his first rodeo. Mr. Larson, Billy, and Rob pulled the horse trailer in one vehicle; and Sylvia, her mother, and Grandfather rode along in another. As they rode along, Billy and Mr. Larson explained how everything would go. Sylvia would get up to three rides; the first two runs would be elimination runs, getting down to the finals of the barrel racing event. Since Sylvia was only seventeen, she could have chosen to run in the junior competition; but she had chosen to run in the open, which meant she would be going up against some of the best riders in the state. Mr. Larson told Rob that Sylvia had been competing since she was a young girl, and she was considered one of the top barrel racers around. Rob had already figured as much from the trophies and ribbons back at the ranch.

The rodeo would officially begin at noon. They were getting there by eight o'clock so they could get the horse situated and Sylvia would get the opportunity to make some practice runs sometime in the morning. Billy explained that the practice runs were extremely important so they could figure out how soft or hard the ground was. Sylvia would want some idea of how she would want to make her runs. Firmer ground would allow her to go into the barrels with a little more speed, and she wouldn't have to worry as much about the horse losing its footing. If the ground were loose, she would have to slow the horse down more and stay farther away from the barrels.

All morning long they worked in preparation for the day's events. Sylvia found out she would be making her run at about three o'clock. Everyone agreed that her practice runs went well. The ground seemed firm, and Sylvia began to get more comfortable all the time with Billy's horse. Rob sensed that even Sylvia was beginning to get caught up in the excitement.

At around eleven o'clock, they began the final preparations for the beginning of the rodeo. Sylvia changed into her best western garb, and Billy prepared the horse for its entry into the arena. Billy explained to Rob that all the contestants would enter the arena at noon in what could be described as near pageantry. They would come in and parade around the arena, all dressed up in their western regalia.

...

Rob and the rest of the family made their way into the stands a little before noon, while Billy stayed behind to help Sylvia with any last minute preparations for the horse. Rob couldn't believe the sense of pride he felt when the contestants finally made their way into the arena. Even the horses seemed to sense the moment, for Rob watched in amazement as they seemed to prance around the arena as they passed in front of the grandstands.

Time seemed to pass quickly by until it was finally nearing the time for Sylvia to make her first run. Mr. and Mrs. Larson explained to Rob how things stood so far. Sylvia would need to finish in the top twenty-five positions today to move into the second round tomorrow. So far, Mr. Larson said, the times were very good and Sylvia would have to have a really good run to get into the second round. He said she'd need somewhere around a 16.5 second run to continue on the next day.

Finally, the time had come for Sylvia to complete her run. Rob couldn't believe the butterflies he felt in his own stomach. He couldn't imagine how Sylvia must be feeling right now. He didn't think he could even sit in the saddle. Then he heard the announcer call her name over the speaker system. The people in the stands cheered as they announced that she was a local girl.

Rob waited anxiously until, suddenly, Sylvia burst into her run. Mr. and Mrs. Larson, Rob, and Grandfather all stood and seemed to hold their breath collectively. She turned sharply around the first barrel and headed toward the second. She seemed to fly around the second barrel and head for the final barrel. In no time she went cleanly around the last barrel and headed toward the finish line. Sixteen-four flashed upon the screen and Mr. and Mrs. Larson both screamed. It was the lowest time posted so far. They told Rob that would surely get her into the second round.

They made their way back to where Sylvia and Billy were waiting. When they got there, Rob was glad to see that Sylvia was as excited as everyone else. They were all talking about what a great run it was. They continued to all talk as Billy and Mr. Larson began to take the saddle off the horse and to brush it down.

Rob was so excited about the rodeo that he wanted to stay and watch it all, but they decided they'd stay until all the times were posted to see what time Sylvia would make her run tomorrow and then they would head home.

When the times were finally posted, Sylvia found she had run the second fastest time of the day. She also found out that she would ride again at about two o'clock on Sunday. Everyone was congratulating her; but when she replied that she needed to squeeze a little more speed out of the horse, both Mr. Larson and Billy told her that she only needed to run her race and to not be concerned about the other times.

"You ran a really good time today, Sylvia. If you post that time tomorrow, you should be able to win this thing. You don't need to do anything differently," Mr. Larson told her.

"I agree completely," Billy reiterated. "You ran a great time. That could easily be the winning time tomorrow. For one thing as that ground is torn up more, if anything, times will get slower. You just run your race."

Billy then told them that he'd get up to the grounds early in the morning to feed and take care of the horse and everyone else could get there around one o'clock to get ready for Sylvia's next run. "I want you to be rested and ready to go," he said as he smiled at Sylvia.

...

Sunday morning came, and Rob went down to have breakfast with the family. "Why Rob, you sure do look nice this morning," Mrs. Larson exclaimed.

"Do you guys think I could go to church with you this morning?" he asked.

Everyone turned to look at him momentarily. Rob had not gone with them all summer long. It was a time he usually spent with Grandfather, and he always enjoyed their Sunday mornings together. But today he wanted to be with the family.

"Sure," Mr. Larson replied. "I hope you won't be too disappointed, but we are planning to come home a little early anyway to get ready for this afternoon."

"Well," Rob replied, "I guess we can cut short my first trip into the church."

By one o'clock they were all back at the rodeo grounds preparing for Sylvia's next ride. When the time came for her second run, Rob couldn't believe how nervous he was. He thought he had been anxious yesterday, but that was nothing compared to today. This time when Sylvia's name was called, they were already standing and cheering.

Again, the horse shot forward with a burst of speed. Sylvia ran through the course with the same intensity as the previous day, and everyone cheered when they saw 16.45 flash across the clock. Once again, that was the best time they had seen posted so far, and over half the riders had already gone.

"That should do it!" Mr. Larson exclaimed. "That should get her into the finals.

By the time the other riders had gone, two others had finished with lower times. Sylvia found out that she would be running in the finals around eight o'clock. And Sylvia, once again, was worried about the riders who had finished with quicker times. But both Billy and Mr. Larson were telling her again not to get caught up thinking about the lower times. "Just run your race" was what they were both telling her.

"The arena's getting more torn up all the time," Billy said. If anything, you might want to slow it down a notch."

"Are you kidding!" Sylvia replied. "I didn't come here to finish anywhere but first. I know what I'm doing out there."

"Well, I just think everyone's going to be slowing it down a little. If you run even close to what you just ran, you're going to win this thing. But now I want to get the saddle off this horse and get it some rest before it runs again. You should get some rest too."

The time 'til Sylvia's final run flew by. In no time, Sylvia and Billy were down preparing for her final run and Rob and the rest of the family were waiting anxiously in the stands.

This time when Sylvia's name was called over the speaker system a hush came over the crowd. As Billy had predicted, the times so far had been slower than earlier in the day. Rob was thinking that if she could only run as well as she did earlier, she would win.

Sylvia took off hard. She bore down on the first barrel and flew around it. She tore around the second barrel and seemed to be riding even more quickly than earlier in the day. She raced toward the final barrel and turned hard to make it around. It was then that the whole crowd seemed to moan. Everyone saw the horse's front hooves lose their footing as it tried to go around the final barrel. From then on it all seemed to be in slow motion for Rob. The horse continued to slide as its hind legs also flew out from under it. Sylvia's forward momentum sent her hurtling over the horse. The horse rolled completely over and quickly jumped back to its feet as Sylvia plowed face first into the dirt. She lay there for a moment without moving. A hush fell over the crowd. Rob saw Billy, along with others, running out toward her. Then she rose, and the crowd began to clap, thankful that she wasn't hurt. It was all over.

When Rob and the rest of the family got down to where the horse was stabled, Rob could hear Sylvia and Billy arguing.

"I told you that you didn't have to take it so fast, but you just had to run her all out. You could have won," Billy was saying.

"Golden Boy would have made that turn. He would have won." Sylvia was shouting back at him.

"Hey, it wasn't my horse's fault you were thrown."

When Mr. and Mrs. Larson got there, Sylvia and Billy both turned away from each other.

"Hey, you did a great job, both of you," Mrs. Larson said consolingly.

"Look, you made it into the finals with a horse you'd never really ridden before. You both should be proud," Mr. Larson said.

...

Throughout the drive home, Sylvia sat quietly. Rob had hoped she would be glad to have ridden in the rodeo no matter what the outcome. But he soon realized that riding Golden Boy in the rodeo meant more to Sylvia than he could have ever imagined. His hope that all his sins would be washed away through the rodeo was now vanquished.

Chapter 14

It **had been two weeks** since the rodeo, and Sylvia still wasn't talking to Rob. All summer long he had wanted to take a ride up in the mountains, and now that he knew he would be leaving on Saturday, he was even more anxious to go. Rob knew that there was no way that Sylvia would take him, so his only hope was to ask Mr. Larson to take him. Rob waited until they had finished their meal, and they were ready to start clearing the table. And he said, "Mr. Larson. I know I've been a lot of trouble, and I would understand if you say no. But all summer I've been dying to ride up into the mountains on a horse. Could you possibly take me?"

"Well, Rob. I'd like to, but I have a lot of work to do tomorrow. And, anyway, do you think you're ready for that long of a ride? That's an eight-hour ride, four up and four back."

Sylvia looked down and smiled. She was sure her father wouldn't take Rob up to the lake in the mountains. She was somewhat glad he wouldn't get to go.

"I think I've gotten pretty good at riding around here, and

I've about been everywhere there is to go on horseback on the ranch." Rob answered.

"Yes, but riding around the ranch is a lot different than riding up the mountain. And being on a horse for eight hours isn't near as easy as you might think."

When Grandfather spoke, it seemed to surprise everyone. Rarely did he speak at the supper table. "One can learn a lot about oneself on a ride into the mountains. I think he is ready."

Mr. Larson looked at Grandfather for a moment puzzledly. After all these years together, he still hadn't figured that old man out. "Well, if Grandfather thinks you'll be okay, I don't see how I can refuse. However, there is no way I can take you tomorrow, but I don't see any reason why Sylvia couldn't take you."

Sylvia's head jerked up, and she nearly shouted, "But I don't want to take him. Why should I? I won't do it."

Mr. Larson turned toward Sylvia and said sternly, "Young lady. You will not speak that way at our dinner table. I didn't ask you if you wanted to. You don't have anything to do tomorrow, and there is no reason you can't take Rob. He is still our guest here, and you will treat him as such."

Grandfather stood abruptly and said, "Sylvia, would you come into my room please?" He turned and headed toward his room. Sylvia rose and followed him, looking around the room. Never had her grandfather done such a thing, and she didn't know what to expect.

As she was walking away, her father said, "And Sylvia, why don't you go ahead and bring Big Red and the bay into the barn tonight so you won't have to catch them in the morning."

Then Mr. Larson turned back to Rob. "You'll need to gather your things tonight and get it all packed because you'll need to leave at first light if you want to get back before sunset."

"What's there to pack?" Rob asked.

"You should never go into the mountains unprepared." Mr. Larson said. "You never know what kind of weather you'll get into at that elevation. Why, it can snow in the middle of the summer. And at this time of year you'll get a thunder shower just about every afternoon, and many times it'll hail. There're bears up there too, and you'll be going over some very rough ground. You fall off your horse up there, and you've got a problem. And it's always better to have something and not need it than to need it and not have it. Plus, you are planning to fish, aren't you? We'd all love to have some fresh trout for supper tomorrow night. Come on. Let's get the kitchen cleaned up and then I'll help you pack."

They had just finished cleaning the kitchen when Sylvia came out of Grandfather's room. She walked up to her father and said, without glancing at Rob, "I'll go on out to the pasture to get the horses." Rob wanted to say something to her, but he didn't know what to say.

Grandfather didn't come out of his room with Sylvia, and both Mr. Larson and Rob wondered what he had said to her. Mr. Larson seemed to not know what to say either, even though he too was very curious about the conversation that took place; for all he said was, "Good. Rob and I are going to go out to the tack room to get the supplies ready."

Then Sylvia asked, "Would it be alright if I took Dizzy instead of the bay?"

Her father furrowed his brow and said, "I'm not so sure Dizzy is ready for a ride into the mountains. I think she's still too green."

"I know I can handle her," Sylvia replied, "and she's got to learn some time."

"I really don't know if now is the right time, but I guess you can take her if you think she's ready. And Big Red will have a calming influence on her. But feed them well tonight so they won't be trying to eat tomorrow."

"I know that, Father." Sylvia bounded out the door to get Dizzy and Big Red, and Mr. Larson and Rob started out to the barn.

When they got to the tack room, Mr. Larson started getting things down and organizing them on the floor. Rob had always wondered why they had all that stuff in there. Mr. Larson got down two parkas, two saddlebags, two bedrolls, a tarp, a rope, a small first aid kit and a large knife in a sheath that he stuck in one of the saddlebags, two small rods and reels, and a small tackle box.

"If I were going, we'd take fly rods; but I don't think Sylvia is going to want to take the time to teach you how to fly fish tomorrow."

"Sylvia can fly fish?" Rob asked.

"Nearly as well as I can," Mr. Larson replied. "She's been fishing since she was big enough to hold a rod."

"Why do we need all this stuff?" Rob asked.

"Well, the parkas are in case it rains. You'll put some food for the day in the saddlebags, and we have a little cooler that fits in one for you to put the fish in. Of course, you'll have to clean them up there." Before Rob could say anything, Mr. Larson said, "Don't worry. Sylvia knows how to clean them. And as I said before, the weather can get very crazy up in the mountains, so you should always have a bedroll with you. If the temperature drops and you get stranded, you can get hypothermia even in the summer."

"What's hypothermia?"

"That's where your body temperature gets too low. You see, it can get down below freezing at night at that elevation even in the summer."

"But we're not going to be there at night."

"As I said, though, it's safer to have it. And you should always have rope, a first aid kit and a knife with you. Now, you'll want to pack a change of clothes with you too. You can count on it being in the 40's in the morning and warming up to the 70's by midday."

"Why will I need a change of clothes?"

"If it comes a hard thunderstorm, you aren't going to want to stay in wet clothes the rest of the day. Even with the parka you'll probably get soaked, and you'll be freezing by the time you get home. And you'll want to take layers of clothes. Take another long sleeve shirt and a windbreaker along too. If I were going, we'd take along a pack horse and spend the night."

"Well, why don't you go?" Rob asked.

"I have too much work to do around here tomorrow. Maybe we can go up there soon and spend a couple of days. I haven't done that in a while, and I need a break."

Rob looked down and replied, "Well, I'm going home on Saturday, ya know, and I don't know if I'll be coming back." Mr. Larson looked at him and didn't say anything.

By the time they had finished packing everything, Sylvia was leading the two horses into the barn. "Why don't you feed them plenty of oats tonight, so they won't be too hungry tomorrow. There's nothing more aggravating than an animal constantly wanting to stop and eat as you're riding along," Mr. Larson told Rob. "Carry your saddlebags up to the house, and you can pack some food and other supplies in there. You'll wrap your clothes up with the bedroll and parka and tie them behind the saddle. Keep the parka separate from the clothes so you can get to it easily in case it starts raining on the trail."

When they got back to the house, Sylvia and Rob went to the kitchen to gather supplies for the trip. She got out beef jerky from the freezer that they made there on the ranch. Rob really liked it, and he and Sylvia had gotten it often for their rides around the ranch. But they hadn't been riding together since the fire.

Rob had always enjoyed their rides. In fact, he couldn't think of anything he had ever enjoyed more. They each prepared a canteen of water, and Sylvia explained that they could fill the canteens from streams up in the mountains. But they did have to add purifying water tablets just to be safe. They also packed some fruit for the trip. Finally, Sylvia got out a small, soft cooler that would hold any fish they caught. She put it in the freezer along with a few small packs of blue ice and explained that they would keep the fish fresh on the trip home.

Sylvia then said that they had better get to bed. She would wake him at 4:30 a.m., and they would need to leave at 5:30 a.m. This was the most Sylvia had said to Rob since the fire, and the first time she had spoken to him since then without sounding angry. As he started up to his room, Rob wondered what Grandfather had told her. But the excitement of tomorrow soon made him forget all about Sylvia and her grandfather. He was finally taking that trip up into the mountains.

Chapter 15

Four-thirty came way too early for Rob. He couldn't believe how excited he was, and his excitement had kept him up much of the night. He knew that he had not slept over four hours, but he was soon wide awake, thinking of his adventure ahead. Nearly all summer long he had wanted to ride up into the mountains, and now he was finally getting to go. He also had another reason for wanting to go today; he wanted to prove to Sylvia that he had changed.

He got dressed and went on down the stairs to the kitchen. There he found Sylvia already up and moving about. Rob could smell the coffee brewing. A nice cup of coffee in the morning had become another one of Rob's rituals since he had come to Montana.

"Good morning, Sylvia," he said as cheerfully as he could, wanting to set the mood for the trip.

"Good morning," she replied with hardly any emotion whatsoever. "I see that you managed to get up without me calling you. That's good."

"Yeah, I think I hardly slept thinking about today. I really want to thank you for taking me. I. . . ."

"Look, it's no trouble," Sylvia cut him off in mid-sentence and continued moving about the kitchen, seemingly trying to stay busy so she wouldn't have to talk to him.

Rob stood there watching her. "Well, thanks again. Is there anything I can do to help?"

"No, but you should go ahead and eat soon so we can get on our way. As soon as the sky starts to lighten we ought to head out." Sylvia moved over to the coffee pot, picked it up and poured coffee in the cup she had set out. "The coffee's ready if you want a cup."

Rob moved over toward her. "Sure," he said. Sylvia set the coffee pot down, moved out of the way, and let Rob pour his own cup. Well at least she set a cup out for me, Rob thought.

Rob turned toward Sylvia and said, "I think I'll drink my coffee out on the porch. Care to join me?"

"No thanks," Sylvia replied; "I need to finish up in here, and then I want to saddle the horses."

"Well, I'll help you saddle and pack up the horses after I finish my coffee and get a bite to eat. How long till we'll be leaving?"

Sylvia didn't look at Rob while she was talking. He thought to himself that she was only doing busy work to keep from facing him. He was trying his best not to show that his feelings were hurt and to stay cheerful. As she was packing the saddlebag, Sylvia said, "I think it will be light enough for us to start by 5:15; and I'm sure no later than 5:30. We'll just be passing through the pastures for a while. By the time we get into the tree line we should have plenty of light."

'Well, that's a start,' Rob thought. 'That's the most she's

said to me in two weeks.' "Good," he called as he was opening up the door. "That gives me plenty of time to drink my coffee and eat something. Then I'll help you with the horses."

Rob walked on out into the brisk morning air. The cool mornings still amazed Rob. Here it was in the middle of the summer, and it couldn't be over 45 degrees. The night sky was amazingly clear. Rob could easily make out the Milky Way stretching across the sky. He had never even seen the Milky Way before he had come up here. In California he could hardly ever even make out any stars. He had never really thought of looking up into the night sky. Now it was one of his favorite things to do. He had never seen a shooting star before coming to Montana. Now he saw them almost every time he went out at night, which was often.

He had been out a lot since the fire. It gave him some time to think in solitude, and he'd done a lot of thinking. Rob now knew what he wanted to do. The thought had begun to form in his mind before the fire, but now he was sure of it. Only now he didn't know if it would ever be possible. He saw it as a long shot even before the fire. Now . . . ?

The figure appearing before him startled him so badly he nearly dropped his coffee cup. He started to turn to run, but then he recognized. . . .

"Grandfather! What are you doing out here?" Rob exclaimed.

"I am always out here in the morning." The old Indian smiled at him. "Why do you think I go to bed so early? Do you think I sleep my life away like some teenager? I come out as you have—to enjoy the morning sky. There is nothing more beautiful than the morning. Come. Take a walk with me."

"But I have to help Sylvia get things ready, and I haven't eaten yet," Rob replied.

"We will only be a moment. Come." And with that the old man started walking away from him. Rob saw he had no choice but to follow. They set out on the trail that headed down toward the stream. The old man walked along in the darkness as though he could see the trail perfectly. Rob walked along trying to emulate the old man but found it hard to keep from feeling his way along the trail. Rob knew that there were rocks all along the path and yet the old man walked along seemingly not even paying attention to the trail before him. Rob couldn't help but marvel at the ease with which the old man moved.

"So you will journey to the mountains this morning, my son. What do you expect to find there?" Grandfather asked.

"I really don't expect to find anything there. I've just wanted to go up there since I got here." Rob said.

"Ah, I think not," said the old man. "When you first got here, you did not even see the mountains. You only wanted to get back to your home, not travel farther away from it."

Rob smiled. "Yeah, you're right. I guess I didn't even see them. But they're not really any farther away. Actually, I think they're even a little closer to California," Rob said with a little bit of pride in his newfound sense of direction.

The old man turned and faced Rob and said in a near whisper so that Rob had to lean forward to hear him, "No, you are wrong. The mountains are a long way from your old life. Further than you would ever believe. The mountains will make your old life disappear and a new one will emerge. Tread carefully today, son." As he finished speaking, he stared at Rob with his head only inches from the boy's until Rob finally had to turn away.

It took a moment for Rob to gather his thoughts. Then he kind of shook his head, laughed and said, "Why are you always doing things like that to me? Geez, sometimes you scare the you know what out of me."

Then the old man smiled and said, "But sometimes one listens best when he is scared." The old man turned serious again as quickly as he had just smiled. "So, heed my advice. Remember the things I have taught you. Your destiny is held by those mountains." And he pointed to the peaks behind him. "I have seen this."

Rob now stared at the old man, not wanting to take his eyes off him. "I will, Grandfather. I'll be very careful. But now I need to get back and help Sylvia prepare for the trip." With that, Rob turned and headed toward the house.

When he entered the kitchen, Sylvia was still busying herself there. Rob quickly began to make his breakfast, all the while thinking about the old man's words. What could the old man possibly have seen? Or was he only telling Rob this? Rob smiled to himself as he thought about the strange old man he had grown so close to.

Sylvia pulled him out of his trance when she asked him if he was ready to get started.

"Sure," Rob said as he jumped up excitedly. Sylvia put her hand up and stopped him, looking around the room as she did so.

"Look, I've got to tell you. I know you are excited about this trip, but I'm not. I'm only taking you because I have to. I'll go, but don't expect me to do so cheerfully."

Rob looked at her for a second. He thought about telling her to just forget it. He thought about telling her that if she felt that way, then it wasn't worth going; but he didn't. This was his one chance to show her he'd changed. She meant too much to him now for him to give up that easily. The old Rob would have given up and acted like he didn't care, but he did care. Instead he said, "Sure, I understand how you feel, but I've got to see the mountains before I leave here; and this will probably be my only chance. I won't be too much trouble. I promise. Who knows? You might end up having fun. At least I hope so."

Sylvia mumbled something that Rob didn't quite hear as she turned toward the door, and then she said, "Well, let's carry this stuff out and take off."

With that she picked up one of the saddlebags and headed out the door. Rob picked up the other one and followed after her. They walked on down to the barn in the early morning light and in a little while had the horses saddled and ready to go. Rob remembered what Mr. Larson had said and put the rain parka in a place he could get to easily. They were out of the barn and headed through the pasture toward the mountain trail by 5:20 a.m., ahead of schedule.

They walked the horses easily across the fields, the elevation slightly rising. The morning air was brisk, and dew covered the fields. A mist came out of the horses' nostrils as they breathed. Rob was so excited he could hardly contain himself. He admired the way Sylvia carried herself in the saddle. She seemed to be one with the animal, he thought. It was almost rhythmic the way they walked along. Rob thought if he closed his eyes he could see a small band of Indians making their way up toward the mountains. He wanted to start chanting as Grandfather had shown him, but he didn't know what Sylvia would think; so they rode along in silence.

They rode for twenty minutes before they were off the Larsons' ranch. Now they exited the fields onto national forest land. They had been steadily climbing since leaving the barn. The open pasture land had long since given way to pine forests and aspen groves. Now the forests were getting thicker, and they were climbing more steeply. Rob found himself having to lean forward in the saddle as they climbed the mountain. The horses still lumbered along easily, but the ground was getting much rockier and the trail less easy.

Sylvia stopped suddenly and pointed off to her right. Rob looked out and saw a mule deer in a small meadow. Its antlers were still growing, and it had not yet rubbed all the velvet off. Grandfather had shown him trees along the meadows below near the ranch where the deer had rubbed the bark off. Grandfather had told Rob how you could find the trails the deer used by looking for the rubs on the trees. Rob smiled as he thought of how Grandfather had told him to follow the deer trails when he walked through the forest because there would not be bears or mountain lions along these trails. The deer would avoid those areas if there were. Rob never knew whether the old Indian was just teasing him or if he really meant these suggestions as advice, but Rob had always listened; and he had always learned.

Sylvia started to lead the way up the trail again. She turned and spoke quietly to Rob: "It's about time to rest the horses, but we'll go on ahead to the next meadow so we don't disturb the deer. There's a stream that follows this trail down the mountain. We'll let the horses get a drink and rest for a while. They have a long day ahead of them." Then she pulled on in front of Rob and continued up the trail. Rob thought to himself that this ride just might work. That was the first time since the fire Sylvia had spoken to him without the anger in her voice. They continued slowly up the trail.

The sun was now in full view, and the morning was finally warming when Rob saw another clearing up ahead. Sylvia saw it at about the same time and pointed. When they got into the meadow, Sylvia dismounted and started pulling the saddlebags and pack roll off the horse. Rob dismounted and did the same. "We'll pull their saddles off and give them a breather for a while," Sylvia said. "They won't go anywhere, and they can graze a little and get a drink in peace. We'll rest about thirty minutes and then hit the trail."

"That sounds great to me." Rob said. When he had dismounted, he had noticed a little soreness in his seat. And we've only been riding for about an hour and a half, he thought.

They sat in silence there in the meadow. The forest around them was alive with sounds, birds singing, chipmunks chattering. Rob made out a dove calling mournfully in the distance. To think that less than three months ago he didn't even know what a dove sounded like. Now he could recognize its call even at a great distance. The cacophony around them, though, only heightened Rob's awareness of the silence between them. Rob desperately wanted to speak to Sylvia, to tell her how he felt, to tell her about the emotions that were welling up inside him.

Finally, he began, "Listen, I want to tell you how sorry I am."

"Rob, I really don't want to hear it. Okay? I'm not ready. Right now, I still feel so mad at you, and I just don't want to hear it." She turned her head away from him and looked out across the meadow.

Rob started to continue but thought, 'What's the point right now?' The old Rob would have given up, but the new Rob wasn't going to. He had to get Sylvia to understand how sorry he was and that he had changed. It was too important to him to give up. But he could see that now wasn't the time.

As he looked around at their beautiful surroundings, he thought, 'How can she stay mad in a setting like this?' They were in a meadow that covered approximately two acres. A gentle breeze blew down the mountain. Wildflowers covered the meadow and gently rocked in the breeze. The grass swayed rhythmically. The meadow was nestled in amongst an aspen grove, and the silver leaves of the aspens fluttered in the wind. Rob lay back and took in the beauty of his surroundings. He looked over at Sylvia and thought that he could see the tension leaving her face. How could it not, he thought.

He closed his eyes and Grandfather's words rolled across his mind–"The mountains are a long way from your old life. . . .Tread carefully. . . ." Rob smiled to himself. He loved that strange old man. But what could he have meant? Rob lay still and let the clouds drift over him.

It seemed like no time at all before Sylvia got up and told him it was time for them to move on. They hadn't staked the horses but had let them graze about in the meadow. But as soon as Sylvia whistled, their heads raised and they started quickly walking toward her. In no time they were mounted and on their way again.

Rob was thinking that the trail was getting steeper when Sylvia said, "Okay, this is where it starts getting a little more difficult. Make sure you always have a good grip on the reins. Sometimes the horses will lunge a little to get up a steep section, so don't worry about grabbing the saddle horn if you need to. You don't want to go right off the back."

They entered another aspen grove on the other side of the meadow. The trail they were following seemed no more than a game trail to Rob. He couldn't help but wonder how Sylvia knew her way. But he wasn't about to ask her if she knew where she was going. He had grown to appreciate her knowledge of the woods. He had no doubts that she knew what she was doing; he trusted her!

The horses made their way up the scant trail, occasionally stumbling as they went. Patches of snow now appeared in the shady areas. Rob noticed a difference in the air; it was lighter, cooler, almost cool enough for his heavier jacket. Rob realized what Sylvia had meant now about keeping a good grip on the reins. Riding a mountain trail differed completely from riding around the ranch. Occasionally his horse would lunge ahead to climb an embankment or a steep section of the trail, sometimes slipping on loose rocks.

A calm overtook Rob that he hadn't felt in ages, maybe ever. He started to feel as one with the horse and saddle. He let his body relax and go with the movement of the horse. He swayed with the movement. The gentle swaying relaxed him even more.

For two more hours they rode along, hardly speaking the whole way. Finally, the climb began to level off. There was snow almost everywhere there was shade. Before them a large, open meadow appeared, and a lake glimmered in the near distance. Only in pictures had he ever seen anything like this. He caught a smile flashing across Sylvia's face. Even she could not resist the beauty before them.

"We have a spot over to the west where we usually fish. There's a spot there where we can start a fire too. We'll eat our lunch first, have some hot cocoa, and then I'll teach you how to fish for trout. I brought along my fly rod for me to use."

Rob could hardly contain his smile. He knew it. Sylvia was almost enjoying herself now. For the next few hours Rob and Sylvia enjoyed the mountains. Sylvia tried to teach Rob how to fly fish, but he finally gave up and used a rod and reel. They caught all the trout they could carry home, and Sylvia cleaned them and prepared them for the trip back to the house. Rob had never even caught a fish before, let alone cleaned one. Since it was nearly three o'clock and they hadn't eaten since ten that morning, Sylvia decided to cook a couple of the trout for them to eat before they started back down the mountain. Rob explored around the lake's edge a little longer while Sylvia cooked the trout.

When he came back up to the fire, Rob noticed Sylvia staring off to the north with a look of apprehension. Rob looked back and discovered large, dark clouds rolling toward them.

"What's wrong?" He asked.

"Those clouds just don't look too friendly," Sylvia replied.

"But I thought your dad said storms come through here almost every afternoon?"

"They do, but they usually form up here over the mountains. This one is different. It's rolling in from the north. We call them Blue Northers around here, and they can get pretty bad. We better pack our gear and get out of here." With that, she was already up and moving, assembling their supplies and packing them away. "It was time to get started anyway since we wanted to get home before dusk."

In no time they were on the trail and headed home, but they could already hear the thunder echoing behind them. Big Red didn't seem to be too disturbed, but Sylvia could tell that Dizzy was getting anxious. She started speaking to her gently to ease her nerves and to let her know everything would be fine. Sylvia breathed a sigh of relief when they left the open meadow and entered the forest. She didn't want to be out in that meadow when the lightning started. The mountains can be a very dangerous place in a lightning storm.

It soon started to sprinkle, so Rob and Sylvia both untied their parkas from the saddles. As the storm moved closer, each clap of thunder seemed louder than the previous one, and Dizzy was getting more anxious and harder to control. Sylvia was doing everything she could to keep her on the trail and to keep her moving along. Rob was beginning to get a little anxious himself. He had begun to appreciate these summer lightning storms down at the ranch. He'd seldom seen anything more beautiful than a storm moving across the mountain range, but being out in the middle of one was a completely different matter. He could see that Sylvia was having an increasingly hard time keeping Dizzy under control.

Rob was about to ask Sylvia if she thought they should stop for a while when a brilliant flash of light burst before his eyes and immediately there was a tremendous clap of thunder. What happened next he would never forget for the rest of his life. It was as if it all happened in slow motion. He saw Dizzy rear up on her haunches, catching Sylvia completely off guard. The bolt of lightning had struck only a few feet from her and had temporarily stunned her. Rob would never forget the startled look in her eyes. He heard himself hollering, "NNNOOOO!" Then he saw Sylvia go airborne up and over the rump of Dizzy, and Dizzy bolt down the trail before them. Rob saw Sylvia hit the ground, and he heard a sickening thud. She seemed to bounce a couple of times, and then she lay there lifeless. Rob first thought about going after Dizzy, but something about Sylvia's lifeless body told him that finding Dizzy was not a priority.

Rob jumped off his horse, quickly tied it up so that it couldn't run away, and ran over to Sylvia. The rain began to fall harder, but for the moment he didn't even notice. He wanted to grab her and shake her and to ask her if she was all right, but he quickly remembered that an injured person shouldn't be moved until you know what is wrong. He called her name several times, and Sylvia didn't respond at all. At least he could see that she was breathing. She was alive! Thank God.

Rob's heart was beating so hard he could hear it, and he was afraid it was going to burst. Panic began to sweep over him. He had no idea what he needed to do. He jumped up and looked around as if to find someone else to help him. Dizzy was nowhere in sight. "God, what'll I do?" He said out loud to himself. Then, it was as though he heard Grandfather's voice saying, "Stay calm and think."

"Yeah, stay calm and think. That's what I need to do." Rob whispered to himself. "Stay calm and think." The rain started to come down harder. "The tarp, I need to get the tarp and get us out of the rain." Rob grabbed the supplies off of Big Red. Luckily, Red was a much bigger horse than Dizzy, so he was packing most of the supplies. Hail began to hit the ground around them. He still wondered what to do about Sylvia, but he said to himself, "First things first. Let's keep dry."

First, he laid the tarp over Sylvia, and then he anchored the back of it on the hill above her with a few heavy stones. This, he thought, would keep the water from running down on to her. Then he took rope and strung it from some nearby trees to the other side of the tarp. In no time he had a roof above them to keep them out of the rain. He had finished their impromptu shelter just in time, for the hail was getting larger and coming down harder. It slapped the top of the tarp so hard that it sounded like rifle shots.

"Wood, I should gather some firewood and place it under the tarp before it gets too wet to burn." There was lots of dead wood around them, so he ran out from under the tarp and started to grab old, dead limbs and to bring them back under their shelter. The hail came down even harder. Luckily, the thick evergreens above them slowed its fall. Even though he was being hit by hail, it wasn't coming down fast enough in the forest to hurt him. He hoped they wouldn't be there long, but he tried to gather enough firewood to get them through the night just in case.

He had been working so frantically that he had hardly realized the temperature had dropped maybe twenty degrees. Suddenly the realization hit him that Dizzy had run off with Sylvia's coat and the other blanket. All they had was his coat and one blanket. He knew that it was important to keep Sylvia warm, so he took both the coat and blanket and spread them over her. As he did so, he noticed her leg. Her boot lay at an odd angle. He knew immediately that Sylvia's leg was broken. "Oh, man, what do I do?" He whispered to himself. Panic started to overtake him again. "Stay calm, stay calm," he started repeating to himself.

It was now almost five o'clock, which meant that they probably couldn't make it back to the ranch before dark even if they had two horses and Sylvia wasn't hurt. Since Sylvia was still unconscious, Rob knew that even if they could somehow start on their way he would have to find the way on his own. He wasn't sure if he could do that in the daylight, and he knew there was no chance for him to find his way when the sun started setting. "Okay," he said to himself, "We're going to be spending the night right here."

He also knew that he had to do something about Sylvia's leg. He had to splint it, and what better time to do it than while she was already passed out. She might not even feel the pain, if she's lucky, he thought. He pulled out his knife and started to cut her jeans from the boot up. When he had cut past the top of the boot, he saw the break. Her leg turned just above the boot. Man, what a bad break, he thought. Luckily, though, it was not a compound fracture. When he was little, someone on his baseball team had gotten a compound fracture during a game. He would never forget that.

So far Sylvia hadn't moved while he was working on her leg. Rob's mind was racing as he thought about what needed to be done. "Her leg's already beginning to swell, so the boot has to come off," he said to himself. "I'll need a couple of pieces of wood and the tape we brought with us. I can set the leg straight and then tape it in place." The thought of doing that sickened him, but he knew it had to be done. The rain was still coming down, but Rob hadn't even noticed it in a while. He went out in search of the wood he would need. Luckily, he had a small axe with the supplies. He decided to cut down a small sapling to use instead of looking around for pieces of dead wood that would work.

Soon he was back under the tarp with the wood and the tape. He stared briefly at the boot, dreading pulling it off. "Maybe I can pull the boot off and set the bone in place at the same time," Rob said still talking aloud to himself. He placed his left hand above the break and took hold of the bottom of the boot with his right hand. He looked up at Sylvia and saw that she had not noticed at all. "Okay, here goes," he said. And with that he pulled the boot off Sylvia. He felt her flinch when he pulled. Luckily, the leg seemed to straighten as he pulled the boot off just as he thought it would. He quickly started to work to tape the pieces of wood to her leg to hold it in place. He had a difficult time trying to hold the wood in place and to wrap the tape around her leg. He had to raise the leg to get the tape underneath; and each time he raised it, Sylvia flinched. "But that's good," he said to himself. "At least I know she has feeling in her legs." He tucked the blanket around her to keep her warm; and then the realization hit him that he was already getting cold, and they would be spending the night on this mountain.

Luckily, he had already gathered enough wood to get a fire going before things had gotten too wet. But he knew he still didn't have near enough firewood to get them through the night. So he set about gathering more wood. He wasn't too worried about the wood being too wet because it hadn't been raining that long, and he knew it would dry around the fire. His parka was keeping most of him dry, but his pants were getting wet, and he was starting to get really cold. He wanted to go build a fire right then and get warm, but he also knew that he had to get things prepared first to spend the night on the mountain.

He cleared out an area under the edge of the tarp to make a fire pit, and he gathered the cooking gear from Big Red. He also took the saddle off the horse and tethered her so she couldn't wander off through the night, but she'd still be able to move around. Soon he had a fire going and was heating water for something warm to drink. He looked around proud of all he had accomplished. He was still extremely worried about Sylvia, but he somehow knew that they were going to get through this.

. . .

Mrs. Larson walked worriedly around the kitchen. Even though no one had said anything, everyone was getting a little anxious. The storm had rolled through over two hours ago, and it was still raining. Normally, it would still be light outside for another hour, but with the dark clouds covering the sky, it already appeared dark. Mrs. Larson was busying herself even though there was nothing for her to do. Mr. Larson kept glancing out the window toward the trail down from the mountains. Only Grandfather seemed to be at ease.

Mrs. Larson's call startled everyone. "Ron! I see a horse with a saddle but no rider." Mr. Larson ran over and looked out the window. Across the field he could make out Dizzy heading toward the barn.

"Get the Sheriff," he called as he was heading out the door. And without another word he was gone. As Mrs. Larson reached for the phone, a hand took hold of hers. It was Grandfather.

"Wait. There is no need to call the Sheriff. We know nothing.

"But something's happened to my little girl. She may need help." Tears were already forming in Mrs. Larson's eyes.

"We know nothing," the old man said again. "Let me go speak to Ron. We must not hurry."

"But who knows what he's done."

"We don't know that he has done anything. I'm sure he would not hurt Sylvia."

Ron burst back through the door. "It was Dizzy. Is the Sheriff on his way?"

"Grandfather told me not to call him," Mrs. Larson replied quietly.

Mr. Larson turned toward the old man. "What?"

"Listen to me, Ron." Mr. Larson found himself thinking that he couldn't remember the old man ever calling him by his name. "The Sheriff cannot help us. He cannot help them. It is nearly dark, and it is raining. We cannot start up the mountain at this time and in this weather. We would not find them, and someone else might get hurt. We must trust that they are okay."

"How can we trust that they are okay? We still don't know anything about that boy. So help me if he has hurt Sylvia, I'll kill him." Mr. Larson could hardly contain himself.

"I know about that boy." Grandfather replied. "And I know Sylvia is safe with him. We must get some sleep so we can leave at first light. Go." And with that the old man turned and headed toward his room. Mr. Larson turned to his wife. They held onto each other and prayed that their child would return to them safely.

"I guess Grandfather is right." Mr. Larson said. "There is nothing we can do right now. At first light I'll saddle up and head up the mountain. I'm sure they had the horses tied up when it started raining and Dizzy just got away. They are probably only waiting out the storm. Let's get some sleep."

...

Rob was huddled close to the fire. He had no idea what time it was, but the storm had passed and the stars were shining brightly above him. Sylvia began moaning and started to move. Rob quickly leaned toward her. She started to rise and cried out in pain. Rob put his arm out to stop her and said, "Shhh, lie back down. Your leg is broken. How do you feel? Does anything else hurt?"

"What happened? My head and my leg are both killing me. Where are we?"

"Lightning struck the tree beside you and you were thrown. Dizzy took off, so I made us a camp right where you had fallen. I was afraid to try to move you. Are you alright?"

"I'm not sure. I feel kind of sore all over. Are you sure my leg is broken?"

"I'm sure. You should have seen it. It was crooked." Rob actually laughed a little. "I tried to set it back in place as best I could."

For the first time Sylvia noticed the pieces of wood taped to her leg. "Well, you're no doctor from the looks of it." Sylvia smiled too as best she could through all the pain. Then she realized that she had on Rob's coat and the blanket was tossed over her while Rob was sitting there without even a sweater by the fire. It had to be down in the upper thirties at the warmest.

"Here, there is enough blanket for the both of us." She held the blanket up and gestured for him to come closer. He hesitated for a moment. "Come on," she said. "I don't bite."

Luckily, the fire had dried him out, so when Rob got the blanket over him, he actually began to warm up a little. "How's the pain?"

"Well, this isn't the first bone I've broken, so I guess it's tolerable. When you've ridden and broken horses all your life, other things seem to get broken too, I guess. How are you doing?"

"Much better now that I'm starting to get warm, and since I know you are all right. You really had me worried there for a while. I couldn't even get a peep out of you. I guess you were out cold."

"Really? How long was I out?" She asked.

"I'm not really sure. You were thrown about four o'clock and it's sometime in the middle of the night now. I guess you were out about eight hours."

"Wow," Sylvia replied. "I had no idea. And you've been right here all this time?"

"Well, I ran down to the mall for a little while, but I came right back." Rob smiled at her. "It's not like I could have left you, now is it. I didn't want to wander off and come back and find you eaten by a bear. Geez, why'd I have to think of bears? Now I have something else to worry about."

Sylvia laughed. "I don't think you have to worry about bears with this fire going."

"Oh, great," Rob said. "Now I have to think about keeping the fire going all night to keep the bears from getting us."

Sylvia laughed again. She wasn't sure if he was joking or serious, but she thought he was joking just to keep her mind off the pain. And it was working. Now they each lay in silence again, and soon Sylvia drifted back off to sleep. Rob was so tired he could hardly think. Now that he was warmer under the blanket, he too soon drifted off to sleep.

...

Both Mr. Larson and Grandfather were up before the first light had entered the sky. Neither of them spoke; both of them knew what had to be done, so they set about preparing for the trip up the mountain. By the time the sky in the east had begun to turn gray, they were saddled up and headed across the field toward the mountain. Even though Mr. Larson wanted to go racing off, he knew that there was no point. The horses would never make it, so they made their way steadily up the mountain.

They had been riding for over two hours, and Mr. Larson was getting more worried. Even if they had lost one of their horses, he thought, they could have started walking from the lake and made it this far along the path by this time. They had kept up a good pace, much faster than Rob and Sylvia would have traveled, and he estimated that they were no more than 45 minutes away from the lake. Where were they?

"Do you smell that?" The old man's words startled Mr. Larson. He stopped his horse and smelled the air.

"No, what?" He asked.

"I smell smoke," the old man replied.

Mr. Larson pulled on the reins and picked up the pace.

Suddenly he smelled it too. It was definitely smoke. Then through the trees ahead he spotted Rob's temporary shelter. He broke his horse into a run.

The sound of hooves beating the ground awakened Rob. He rose up just as Mr. Larson jumped off his horse.

"Boy am I glad to see you."

Rob had barely gotten the words out when Mr. Larson shouted, "Where is she?" with such force that it startled Rob. The look in Mr. Larson's eyes frightened Rob, and he found himself taking a step back.

Mr. Larson looked as though he was about to grab Rob when Sylvia called out, "Dad." Mr. Larson turned toward her. By this time Grandfather had ridden up and quietly dismounted. Rob found himself greatly relieved to see the old man. He ran over and hugged the old Indian.

"Boy, am I glad to see you guys. Sylvia's broken her leg."

Mr. Larson, who had already just about reached Sylvia, stopped in his tracks and turned toward Rob. He looked from Rob to Sylvia for a moment.

"Rob saved me, Daddy," Sylvia said with tears forming in her eyes.

Rob found himself blushing. "No, I didn't. I only did what I had to do," he replied.

Grandfather looked around, at the shelter Rob had built, all the firewood under the tarp, the splint on Sylvia's leg. He noticed Sylvia was wearing Rob's coat and that Rob wasn't wearing one. He noticed everything, and he smiled. Mr. Larson looked at Grandfather; he noticed the old man looking around, and he too took it all in. Soon he started to laugh, and he wasn't sure why. He knelt down and hugged Sylvia. And soon they were all laughing. A great weight had been lifted off them all; they all knew it, felt it.

Then Rob and Sylvia both started to speak, telling the two men of their ordeal. Both of them were speaking excitedly, taking turns telling of their adventure, each filling in the gaps for the other. Grandfather smiled as he sensed the new bond between the two young people. As they tore down Rob's temporary camp, the two continued their story. Soon they were all mounted up, Sylvia riding behind her father, and they were still telling their story.

Sylvia couldn't believe how happy she felt. It was odd for her. Here she was riding along behind her father, her leg broken, pain shooting through her seemingly with every step of the horse, and she was happy. It seemed as though it was no time till they were down the mountain, and then the story began all over again as they recanted the tale to her mother as they were on their way to the hospital.

At the hospital the doctor was impressed with how well Rob had set Sylvia's leg. Many times, he explained, in circumstances such as these, the leg would have to be rebroken and reset; but Rob had done such a good job that they wouldn't need to reset it. Rob beamed with pride. Everyone, even Mr. Larson, was patting him on the back and telling him what a good job he had done.

The doctor examined Sylvia thoroughly and found nothing else wrong with her. He was quite sure she didn't have a concussion, and in a couple of months she would be fine.

Chapter 16

By that afternoon they were back on the ranch. Sylvia had a walking cast on her leg, but she still would have to use crutches for a couple of weeks. And tomorrow was to be Rob's last day on the ranch. Tomorrow he would return to California for the three-month review before the judge.

The Friday night supper routine went as it always did. There may, however, have been a little less talk through the evening meal than usual. The excitement of the past twenty-four hours had passed, and the realization that Rob would be leaving tomorrow had settled upon them all. After supper, the dishes were cleared; and they all moved into Grandfather's room. How Rob had grown to love this room, the distinctive smells, the warmth, the calm. It was a place where Rob always knew he was welcome, and he didn't think that it was his imagination that Grandfather's eyes always seemed to light up when he entered the room. As usual, the room was already prepared for the evening. A small fire burned in the fireplace; the scent of cedar filled the air. Everyone sat silently in the room, waiting for Grandfather to begin. The silence seemed to go on much longer than usual. To Rob it seemed to be even longer than that first Friday evening he had spent in the house. Finally, once again, Rob knew that he could wait no longer. He knew that Grandfather would reprimand him, but he feared that if he didn't speak now the moment might slip away, and he would never have another chance. It was too much of a risk. So he spoke up:

"Excuse me, Grandfather, for my rudeness. May I speak?"

Grandfather stared at him sternly for a moment. Rob expected Grandfather to speak harshly to him for the first time since he had met the old man. Then Grandfather's stern face broke into a smile, and he said, "I have been waiting for you to speak."

Rob couldn't believe the emotion welling up inside of him. He found it hard to speak. Everyone in the room sat looking at him. Finally, he said, "I can't begin to tell you how much these last three months have meant to me. I have learned so much and changed so much. When I came here, I hated this place. Now, I don't want to leave at all. Mr. Larson, I know I've been a lot of trouble for you, but I really think if you gave me the chance, I could be a lot of help around the ranch. What I mean to say is would you consider allowing me to stay here and work on the ranch for room and board? I'm sure you've already spoken to the judge, but would you please reconsider and allow me to stay?"

His heart sank when Sylvia jumped up and ran out of the room as fast as her crutches would carry her. After all they had been through, he had hoped that she had forgiven him. But now he could see that it was useless. How could he have ever thought that these people would want someone like him living with them? He buried his face down in his hands and began to cry like he had never cried before. Eighteen years of disappointments came out in that moment. Eighteen years of sadness welled inside him. Eighteen years of never finding the love that he so dearly craved. Several minutes had passed before he realized that Mrs. Larson was beside him, holding him.

"I thought she had forgiven me." He finally managed to say as he buried his head into Mrs. Larson's shoulder.

Mrs. Larson combed his hair back out of his face and said, "She has forgiven you. She ran out of the room because she was so happy. I think she didn't want you to see her cry. You see, we have already discussed your living with us. Sylvia wanted us to ask you to stay, but Grandfather said it would be better for us to wait and for you to ask us. He said it was all part of your growing up and that he was sure you would ask. As usual, he was correct. We're all so happy that you have decided to stay."

Upon hearing those words another wave of emotion swept over Rob, and he was overcome with tears again. But this time, for the first time in many years, they were tears of joy.

ABOUT THE AUTHOR

Jeff Hammonds is a lifelong educator whose affinity for telling stories in the classroom led to his first novel. He currently lives in Oregon with his lovely wife and their misnamed Australian shepherd/border collie cross, Ares. (He's a lover, not a fighter.) Jeff has lived in the North, the South, Southern California, and the Pacific Northwest, and he brings these different perspectives to life in the characters he weaves into his stories. Enjoy.

CPSIA information can be obtained
at www.ICGtesting.com
Printed in the USA
LVHW051107230620
658651LV00006B/239